Bridesmaid Blues

A Poppy Lewis Mystery

Book 6

Lucinda Harrison

Bridesmaid Blues

Copyright © 2024 by Lucinda Harrison

All rights reserved. No part of this publication may be reproduced, distributed, or transmitted in any form or by any means, including photocopying, recording, or other electronic or mechanical methods without the prior written permission of the copyright holder, except in the case of brief quotations in critical reviews and certain other noncommercial uses permitted by copyright law.

This is a work of fiction. Names, characters, places, and incidents are either the product of the author's imagination or are used fictitiously, and any resemblance to actual persons, living or dead, business establishments, events, or locales is entirely coincidental.

ISBN: 978-1-7367596-5-3

To my best friends. May we endure and never feel compelled to murder one another.

One

THE TOASTER BEEPED one final time, and I stepped back, beaming with satisfaction. I turned to Greta, my aging housekeeper and cook, who retreated against the far wall of the kitchen. "Well?" I asked. "What do you think?"

"Looks like a torture device."

I frowned and turned to the sleek, streamlined toaster atop my countertop. "This smart toaster is supposed to make things easier around here."

"What's so hard about making toast?"

I waved a hand at the brightly lit display and multitude of buttons. "You can pick your own toastiness level. It automatically detects your bread size and adjusts accordingly. It's even voice activated."

Greta didn't move.

"I know you're averse to technology, but this is really cool. So are all the other installations the technician from Smarty Pants Home Solutions made."

A dissatisfied grunt escaped from Greta. "I don't understand why we need a smarty-pants door or smarty-pants lights. Sounds like lazy pants to me."

"At least come take a look at it."

Greta shook her head, and her long, gray hair followed suit. "No chance, Poppy. Besides, it might interfere with The Man's tracking device and make it self-destruct." She wiggled her ankle, and a shiny device clanked with the movement.

I crossed my arms and leaned against the counter. "Your ankle monitor will not self-destruct. You only have to wear it for another month, anyway."

"A month of government servitude. I bet my F.B.I. file is an inch thick by now." She lifted the hem of her long skirt and poked at the bulky device around her ankle.

I held up a hand to block the glint as it caught the sunlight. "Covering it in layers of tinfoil won't protect you."

"Can't hurt." She turned her ankle and admired her handiwork with a grin.

"Well, it's your own fault for trying to hustle the entire town. Illegal gambling and selling liquor without a license are serious crimes."

Greta guffawed. "That's rich. You've seen a murder or three, but my dice games at the local library are *serious crimes*."

I frowned again. "Fine. Serious misdemeanors."

The toaster beeped.

Greta side-eyed it. "Probably recording every word we say."

I let out an exasperated sigh. "It's not recording every—"

Beep.

"Huh." I leaned down to counter level and tapped the

touchscreen. A display with what seemed like a hundred options flashed on the screen. "Cancel," I articulated with a clear voice.

The toaster beeped in response, but nothing changed on the display.

"Maybe I just need to—"

Beep. Beep.

I pressed a button that said OFF. Nothing happened.

Beep.

"Would you please put that thing out of its misery?"

I looked up to see my sister, Lily, sweeping into the kitchen. Her black hair, the same as mine, but still short from regrowth, was swept up in a satin turban. Her eyes were heavily lidded, and she made a direct line to the coffeemaker.

"It's too early for so much noise," she said, then stopped abruptly as she reached the coffeemaker. "What's this? What happened to the old coffeemaker?"

I continued to tap at the toaster screen and the beeping finally ceased, although I'd no idea what I may have pressed to stop it. "It's new. It's a smart coffeemaker."

Lily eyed it with suspicion. "Smart…"

"An agent of government control," Greta said. "Listens to your every word, watches your every move."

Lily peered around the device, giving it a close look. "It can do whatever it wants as long as it makes me a cup of coffee. Is there a manual or something?"

"It's all online," I said. "You need to download the software application and then you can set up your profile with your coffee preferences and everything."

"I just want a cup of coffee."

"Good luck," Greta said with a snort. "You'll need to

disclose your height, weight, religious affiliation, and whether you've ever been a member of the Communist Party."

Lily sighed. "Tea it is, then." She strode across the kitchen, pulled open a drawer, and plucked a dark tea bag from my abundant selection of herbal, green, and black teas. "The kettle isn't smart too, is it?"

"Still dumb as rocks, thankfully." Greta hopped to the stove and placed the stainless steel kettle on the burner.

"What else is smart now?" Lily asked me. "I need a warning, at least."

I cleared my throat. "There's nothing wrong with living in the twenty-first century. This Victorian house may be old, but we can still enjoy modern convenience."

They both stared blankly, appearing unconvinced.

"I've modernized the bed-and-breakfast with smart appliances, lights, and other features. Things my guests will appreciate, unlike you two ungrateful Luddites."

A single eyebrow rose on Lily's face.

I nodded toward my sister. "When is your condo remodel supposed to be completed, anyway? At some point, I'd like my own bedroom back. Sharing with Greta isn't exactly comfortable. Can't you get an apartment or something?"

She waved a delicate wrist in my direction. "I'm waiting for my next collection to release. It's not a good time for transition. You understand, of course."

"And when is that hat collection supposed to come out exactly? It's been quite a long—"

The toaster beeped behind me, and I spun around to face it. "Darn it—"

But at that same moment, a stiff, robotic voice sounded from my phone, which lay nearby on the counter. "Alert. Alert. Front door alert."

Lily sighed audibly. "Smart doors, too?"

"That'll be my guests," I said, brushing invisible dust from the front of my shirt. "A group of bridesmaids and the bride. A full house, so look sharp."

Lily, impeccably dressed in sleek trousers and a soft sweater, smirked, and Greta, stringy hair draped over the drab gray of her long dress, only grunted.

***

I plastered my best smile across my face and swung open the grand front door. Two very different young women greeted me. The first beamed back at me in return. Her wavy blonde hair hung past her shoulders and cascaded down a simple white linen dress. A sparkle hinted in her green eyes and more from the multitude of colorful crystals she wore at her neck and wrists.

"I'm Saffron," she said with a sweet, breezy charm. "And you must be Poppy." She grinned broadly. "I'm the bride."

"Welcome to the Pearl-by-the-Sea, Saffron, and congratulations." I stepped to the side and gestured for the two to enter.

The second woman, tall and statuesque, passed by with a faint waft of jasmine. A glance at her clothing indicated she had money—elegant trousers and a silk shirt of deep, rich green. She brushed her long mahogany waves gently over one shoulder, revealing tasteful emeralds at her ears and a delicate gold necklace. She stepped through the entryway with graceful strides. *Definitely money.*

I glanced out at the porch after they'd passed by and spotted Mayor Dewey, the mayor of Starry Cove, perched on the stair rail post, tail swishing back and forth. He appeared particularly corpulent today. *Too many treats for that cat.*

A hideous hairless dog with about two teeth and a tufted mohawk lolled on the deck nearby. Daisy. They'd grown accustomed to spending their days lazing around the Pearl's grounds. "I have more guests coming, so you two behave."

Dewey blinked one of his slow, sleepy blinks to let me know he was listening but didn't care. At least his tail had stopped twitching.

I closed the door and met the two women inside. Saffron gushed and exclaimed to the other woman, "Isn't it absolutely beautiful, Charmaine? It's so stately and old. And look at this detail." She rushed to the stained-glass panels that flanked the large fireplace and held her arms out wide. She spun around to her companion. "Gorgeous. You'd never see this at Bliss Ridge."

"No." Charmaine leaned casually against the back of a wingback chair. "Definitely not."

"I want to make sure we can catch up with Basil soon, Char. Maybe once everyone's here or first thing tomorrow. It's been so long."

"Basil?" I asked.

"Basil Meyers," Saffron answered. "He's an old family friend. I've asked him to officiate the wedding. That's why we're having the ceremony here in Starry Cove."

"How lovely," I said. "He's just up the road." Pastor Basil Meyers, a little bit hippy, a little bit dippy, ran the nondenominational Fellowship of the Faith church a short way down Main Street. The same church that I'd previously learned concealed somewhere on its grounds the hidden tomb of my ancestor, Claude Goodwin, along with his suspected mounds of pilfered pirate treasure.

"Alert. Alert. Front door alert."

"What was that?" Saffron asked, confused.

"Sorry," I said, fumbling for my phone. "Someone else must be here."

I soon escorted the third arrival, who'd introduced herself to me as Jennifer, future sister-in-law, into the common room. She wore beige separates and her hair was the color of burnt oatmeal. Her appearance was stark next to Saffron's effervescence and Charmaine's quiet elegance. When we entered the grand room, a startled "Oh," escaped from Jennifer's lips. The only response to her arrival from Charmaine was a brief raise of her eyebrow, but Saffron hurried to the beige woman's side.

"Jennifer," she exclaimed, giving the woman a warm hug. "Can you believe this place? I was just saying how different it was from Bliss Ridge."

Jennifer pried herself from Saffron's embrace and set down her bag on a nearby sofa. "You make the commune sound so rustic. Was it really that bad?"

"It wasn't bad at all," Saffron said, "but we didn't have much time for beauty or art between the chores, the gardens, and the animals."

I couldn't hold back my curiosity. "You live on a commune?"

"Lived," Charmaine corrected. "Bliss Ridge. We grew up there. That's how we know Basil Meyers." She held out an elegant hand toward Jennifer and gave her a sly smile. "I don't think we've properly met. I'm Charmaine, Maid of Honor."

Jennifer shook it quickly. "Jennifer. Pleased to meet you."

"Likewise." Charmaine let the word roll slowly from her smirking lips.

"You didn't grow up on the commune?" I asked Jennifer.

"No, my brother and I grew up in the suburbs." Then she lowered her voice so only I could hear. "Like normal people."

Saffron joined in. "Chad's always commenting on how different our upbringings were. Opposites attract, I guess." She let out an airy laugh.

"Chad must be the groom," I said.

"Yes," Jennifer said. "My parents and brother are staying at a luxury resort in nearby Vista." She crossed her arms. "And I'll be staying here with the rest of the bridesmaids."

It was hard not to take this personally, but Jennifer's disappointment at having to stay at the bed-and-breakfast I'd worked so hard to maintain and modernize felt like a punch in the gut. I smiled anyway. "I'm sure you'll find your stay pleasant. The house may be old, but we have all the modern convenience of a luxury hotel. In fact, I've just installed a number of smart features."

Jennifer mumbled something that could have been taken as an affirmation or doubtful resignation.

Charmaine sidled to Jennifer's side, her hips swaying in a fluid motion, and placed one slender arm around Jennifer's shoulder. "She's right, you know," she said, nodding toward me. "You may find your stay quite pleasant."

At that, Charmaine slid away, casting a lingering gaze upon Jennifer, who quickly averted her eyes. Charmaine's lips twisted into a smirk.

"Alert. Alert—" I quickly turned the alarm off.

Saffron started, then clapped her hands in two short bursts. "That must be the others." She grinned at Charmaine, who inclined her head in an acknowledgement, but did not smile in return.

The next arrival introduced herself as Clover, who appeared head-to-toe in branded gear emblazoned with a stylized "Klover Kombucha" covering every inch of her clothing. I even spotted branded earrings beneath her short, curly hair. A hefty crate of glass bottles tinkled as she strained to carry it in her arms.

"Can I help you with that?" I asked.

"Nope," she replied and fumbled awkwardly into the house. "Just need a place to set it down. Precious cargo here. Latest batch of the freshest kombucha you've ever tasted."

"I've never had kombucha."

"Never had…" Clover shook her head. "We'll have to fix that." She set the crate at the foot of the stairwell in the foyer. "I'll need some fridge space to store these bottles."

A high-pitched squeal of Clover's name pierced the air as Saffron bolted from the adjacent common room and threw her arms around the new arrival.

I was soon forgotten as the women fell into reminiscing and introductions, but it wasn't long before the robotic voice alerted me to the next arrival.

Kismet arrived with a sense of reluctance and a slightly furrowed brow that seemed a permanent fixture on her otherwise pretty face. She even hesitated a moment when I gestured her inside before taking the first step of a leaden foot.

"I hope your drive was easy."

"No problem." She set her bag at the foot of the stairs next to the crate of kombucha. "I see Clover's already here."

"Saffron, Jennifer, and Charmaine are here, too."

Her face jolted—just a fraction—then was gone.

"Is everything all right?" I asked.

Kismet shook herself out of whatever deep thought she'd had and quickly replied, "Yes, fine. I was confused by that name. I don't think I've met Jennifer before."

Meeting new people under eventful circumstances was never easy. "I'm sure you'll get along great. She's the future sister-in-law."

"Is that my Kizzy?" Saffron shot from the other room and spun Kismet around before the poor woman could brace herself. "I'm so happy you're here! Poppy," she said to me, breathless, "this is my absolute best, best friend. We've been inseparable since we were babies."

I blinked. *Best friend? Wasn't Charmaine her best friend?*

"We're not babies anymore," Kismet said with a weak smile while peeling herself from Saffron's grip.

"Another commune friend," I said. "What an interesting childhood you all must have had."

Kismet swung tired eyes my way. "You have no idea."

"Alert. Alert. Front—"

A quick stab at my phone shut off the alarm. I'd have to fiddle with the settings later.

A pair of contrasting young women were next through the door. Maya, a dark beauty, wore her black hair in a smart pony tail, like mine, and dressed in comfortable leggings and a stretchy tunic. Heavenleigh appeared as Maya's opposite. Her short, wavy blonde bob blew gently in the salty breeze that crested the cliff side from the ocean below. Her travel wear consisted of loose-fitting linens and thin, billowy cottons. Maya's eyes were deep, dark pools, while Heavenleigh's sparkled like an azure sea. Both were beautiful in distinct ways.

They, too, were greeted with enthusiasm from Saffron in the foyer. Maya squeezed Saffron into a giant bear hug, nearly picking her up off the floor.

"Oof," Saffron said. "I forgot how strong you were."

"It's all the yoga," she replied.

Heavenleigh appeared a bit bewildered by Saffron's hug at first, but she embraced her in return and they both let out a laugh at the same time, giggling at some unspoken memory or simply out of sheer joy at connecting with old friends.

As we entered the common room to join the others, Maya's face turned to stone, and she jerked to a stop at the sight of Charmaine. There was a slight purse of her lips, then her face returned to normal. Charmaine smiled, gently brushed back her hair, and casually fiddled with the jewelry at her ears and neck as though nothing had happened. I knew she must have spotted Maya's initial reaction, but it was hard to tell what else may have passed between them.

Based on snippets of their conversation, I gathered that Maya and Heavenleigh were also friends from the commune days, and they all fell into stories from their youth, chattering away like hens.

To the side, Jennifer sat alone in one of the wingback chairs, swiping at her phone, disengaged from the others' reminiscing. It seemed she was the odd one out in this bevy of bridesmaids.

"Where's Ziggy?" Clover asked the group. "I thought she was coming too?"

As if on cue, my phone once again notified me of a guest at the front door with its jarring robotic alert. Yes, I'd definitely have to fiddle with the settings later.

The aforementioned Ziggy greeted me with a splash of bright white veneers and the telltale surgery-enhanced upturned nose. The saturation of color in her reddish-brown hair told me it came from a bottle.

I gestured her inside, and when she passed, a faint sourness of alcohol wafted along with her.

"This house is amazing," she said with the hint of a slur.

"Thank you." I took her bag and placed it at the foot of the stairs with the others.

"Looks like everyone's here already."

"You're the last to arrive."

She let out a half-laugh. "How dramatic. I guess I'm ready for it."

"Ready for what?" But the answer soon became clear as I escorted Ziggy from the foyer to the common area. The other women, closely huddled and deep in conversation, looked up and let out a collective gasp. Jennifer, still in the wingback chair, leaned aside to get a better look at the new arrival.

"Ziggy?" Saffron's words sounded unsure. "Is that you?"

"What happened to you?" Kismet asked.

As a group—minus Jennifer—they approached Ziggy, who twirled and giggled as they ogled her.

"What do you think?" Ziggy said. "I'm sure I look different, but I assure you it's me."

Kismet touched Ziggy's long hair. "This used to be frizzy."

"And your clothes never looked like mine before." Charmaine reached out and rubbed the fabric of Ziggy's sleeve between two fingers. "Is this silk?"

"I can't believe it," Clover said. "You used to be a runty little thing. Now you look absolutely...stunning."

Heavenleigh made it through the crowd to get her own close look at Ziggy. "My father always said we would each find our time to bloom."

Their voices stilled, and all eyes swiveled toward Heavenleigh.

"How is Papa Zamora?" Saffron's tone was somber.

Maya asked in a whisper, "Has he recovered from the stroke?"

They now crowded Heavenleigh, Ziggy's appearance quickly forgotten.

"He's on the mend," Heavenleigh said, "so wipe those sad looks off your faces. It was minor, and he's already home and resting."

"I shouldn't have asked you here." Saffron hung her head. "You should be home with Papa Zamora."

"Nonsense."

"We should give thanks," Kismet said.

The others nodded, then formed into a circle, arms draped around one another's shoulders. Jennifer and I exchanged confused glances. She shrugged her shoulders.

An intense quiet overtook the space. I held my breath, afraid the slightest exhale would interrupt whatever communal kumbaya was happening in my common room.

The squeaking of the kitchen's swivel door hinges broke the silence. Greta burst through with a tray of fruit. "I set out the—"

I shushed her with a finger to my lips. She twisted her face at my rebuke and dropped the tray onto the buffet with a clamor. "Suit yourself," she whispered harshly, then squeaked back through the kitchen door

A moment later, the huddle broke, although I hadn't heard any words to prompt the separation.

"I can't believe you're all here," Saffron finally said to break the silence. Tears welled in her eyes. "I'm so happy. I just know this is going to be the best week ever."

Two

THREE TRIES LATER and I'd finally managed to toast a few slices of bread to set out with jam for my new guests. The first pair were burnt to coal, and the second felt like hockey pucks.

Greta smirked the entire time as I'd tried to make toast with my new smart machine. "Your smarty-pants toaster's dumber than a dustbin. In the time it's taken you to destroy four slices of toast, I could have had a whole loaf done and devoured."

I pulled slice numbers three and four from the toaster with my tongs and dropped them onto a platter. "Good enough."

"Fantastic. Now cut those two slices into eight tiny pieces and call them *amuse-bouche*. You can serve jam with the world's smallest spoon and they'll never notice that you're slowly starving them to death."

I stripped off my apron and flopped it onto the counter in frustration. "Oh, be quiet, please. We just need to get used to the new machines."

"We?"

"I don't have time for your protests. Grab a bunch of grapes from the fridge and try to make this spread look more appealing."

Greta shut the drawer she'd been pawing through. "Suit yourself. I can't find the tiny spoons, anyway."

We spun through the kitchen door and into the dining space, which sat open to the common room. Greta placed her bowl of grapes on the buffet and I arranged my two slices of toast and jam next to it. I turned the plate a few times, but it still looked like two paltry pieces of toast. "We've set out a few snacks," I said to the women.

"Thank you, Poppy," Saffron said.

I approached the group. All except Jennifer sat together, leaning over a single ottoman covered in loose photographs. "How are you all settling in?"

"Maya brought some old photos and we're going through them. I can't believe how young we all look."

"Or how different," Charmaine said under her breath.

"Look at this one." Saffron snatched one photo from the center and handed it to me. "This is all of us on one of the commune celebration days."

The photograph revealed a line of seven girls, perhaps ten or eleven years old, leaning against a fence wearing poorly crafted paper headbands of varying colors.

Saffron pointed to the headgear. "We made those ourselves."

So much changes from that young age to young womanhood, but I could decipher some of these girls now before me. Maya, straight black hair setting off her mocha skin, was the easiest to spot. Kismet was the shortest, and that tracked as the shortest of the girls, too. Charmaine was the tallest and standing in the middle of the pack like a regal queen. That checked out as well.

"Who is this?" I asked.

Saffron pulled the photo closer, then squinted. "That's Clover, and that's me next to Heavenleigh. Ziggy's on the end."

I checked the photo again. I could barely tell Saffron and Heavenleigh apart with their headbands sitting crooked on their heads and goofy grins plastered on both their faces. But Ziggy. Ziggy was something else. An entirely different person. Frizzy poop-brown hair, frumpy clothes, and skinny knees knocking together like a pair of knobby twigs.

"Incredible, isn't it?" Charmaine's languid voice dripped into my ear. "It's amazing what a transformation she's had."

"And you don't seem to have changed much at all," I said.

Charmaine dipped a shoulder into a cloying shrug.

"She sure hasn't," Maya said. "Charmaine's always been the attractive one and always at the center of everything."

"And Maid of Honor." The sneer in Kismet's voice silenced the room.

"Yes," Charmaine said with a beaming smile. "Maid of Honor."

Saffron spared a quick glare at Charmaine, then walked to the woman she'd called her best friend and locked arms with her. "We're all friends here, Kismet. Let's not spoil it."

Kismet frowned, but said no more.

"How about some kombucha?" Clover's artificially

cheerful voice cut through the air.

"Is it hard kombucha?" Ziggy asked.

"No, but it's still really good. Everyone needs to try it."

"I like the idea of hard kombucha, though." Charmaine tapped a finger to her chin. "Put it on the agenda for the next board meeting, Clover. I want to explore that idea."

Clover's jaw set. It seemed for a moment that she would refuse, but Charmaine's eyes bored into her. Finally, Clover blinked and turned away. "Okay."

"I'd like to try it," Jennifer said. "I've never had kombucha."

"Bring me one, too," Charmaine said.

Clover retrieved a few bottles from the crate in the foyer. Once she returned, she said, "Poppy hasn't had it either." She handed me a bottle, then distributed to Charmaine and Jennifer.

I took a tentative sip and was pleasantly surprised at the subtle fruitiness of it. "This is really good."

"Thanks," Clover said. "I've been working to perfect my recipe for years. If I can get a few more distributers, I really think it's going to take off."

"I'm so proud of you for starting your own business," Maya said.

Clover blushed, then added, "What about you, Ms. Doctor? You're actually saving lives."

Maya smiled, but brushed it off. "We're all doing great things. I can't believe we're back together after so many years."

Jennifer eased deeper into her chair, but Maya spotted her.

"Even you, Jennifer. You're part of this family now, whether you like it or not."

The rest of them laughed, and Saffron leaned down to give Jennifer a gentle hug. Jennifer smiled weakly, but I saw real relief behind her eyes. I had to imagine it was pretty hard to sit there listening to a group reminisce about a past you weren't a part of.

Charmaine raised her kombucha as if to toast. "I agree. Welcome to the family, Jennifer. Here's to the many, many good times we'll have together."

Jennifer shrank back.

"Don't make her feel awkward," Saffron said, then turned back to Jennifer. "I'm glad to finally have a sister. It's something I've always wanted."

"A lovely sentiment," Charmaine said. "Don't you think, Heavenleigh?"

Heavenleigh, who had remained mostly quiet on the fringes of the group, traced her hand along a silver filigree pen holder. She jerked up at the mention of her name. "What's that?"

"Never mind," Saffron said, waving her off. "I want to hear more about what everyone's been up to since we left Bliss Ridge."

Thankfully, my pathetic toast and jam were forgotten, and the women descended into a long evening of anecdotes and grand future plans. With the house full and Greta generally behaving herself, I fell asleep easily that night. No concerns. No qualms. No worries at all.

***

I tugged at the covers, pulling them tighter over my shoulder. Greta snored next to me, occasionally broken by a guttural grunt, wheeze, or fart. She stirred as I tucked the covers under my chin.

My mind wandered back to the short conversation I'd had with Lily that morning and wondered when she'd be moving along and I could finally get my own room back. Sharing a space with Greta was growing tiresome. And smelly.

"Alert. Alert. Front door alert."

Greta shot up in the dark. "Pass the potatoes, Napoleon. They're coming for me!"

"Go back to sleep, Greta. It's just the door alarm."

I checked the time on my phone. Past midnight. Slipping on my robe, I eased open the door to the private suites on the first floor and peeked out into the common room. All quiet.

The alarm from the Smarty Pants app had ceased. "Must have been a false alarm," I mumbled to myself. "Or Dewey slinking around again."

I tossed my robe back onto its peg and crawled back into my cozy, warm spot on the bed. Just as I drifted off to dreamland, the blare of the alarm sounded again.

My hand slapped onto the phone to turn it off, then I eased myself up and threw my robe on. I shuffled into the common room, then through the foyer at the front door. The alarm had stopped again. Through the sidelights flanking the door, I spotted movement close to the base of the porch. Dewey.

As I crept back into bed, I made a mental note to contact the Smarty Pants technician and figure out how to adjust the sensitivity on the alarm. My sanity wouldn't last long if I kept getting jarred awake every time a moth fluttered near the door.

A few minutes later, the alarm went off again. My eyes sprung open, and I glared at the phone.

Greta rolled over. "Would you turn that darn thing off? How am I supposed to get my beauty sleep with all this racket?"

"It's just Mayor Dewey making his rounds."

"Well could he stop rounding near the door?"

I sighed and fell back against my pillow.

Half an hour later, the blare of "Alert. Alert. Front door alert" jolted me from my dream. I slapped the phone, and it tumbled off the side table. "Alert. Alert. Front door alert."

I peeled myself from the warmth of the bed and crouched down to find the phone and turn off the blaring alarm. Through the fog of sleep, I fiddled through the Smarty Pants app trying to find out how to adjust the settings. There were so many options, and I cursed myself for wanting them all, rehashing in my head the conversation I'd had with the technician. *Sure, Mr. Smarty Pants, sign me up for all the bells and whistles.*

I was still holding the phone, methodically working my way through the setting menus, when the alarm sounded again.

"Argh!" I grumbled through my clenched teeth and shook the phone.

A moment later, the door to the small room opened and Lily poked her head in. "Would you silence that alarm? If I don't get my eight hours of sleep, you'll be sorry."

"We'll all be sorry," Greta mumbled from the bed.

"I'm trying to, but I can't find the right setting. The menu is so complicated. I'll have to take a closer look in the morning."

Lily frowned, clearly displeased that I couldn't fix it and ducked away, shutting the door firmly behind her.

I set the phone back on the table and hoped Dewey would move on. It seemed he had because I was finally able to fall back asleep deep into dreaming about my boyfriend, Ryan, riding on the back of a gigantic hairy sasquatch through a dappled redwood forest.

"Alert. Alert—"

Slap!

I peeled my palm off the phone.

Greta heaved herself upright. "If you don't retrieve that cat, I will."

I was already in my slippers and tying the robe around my waist. "I'm way ahead of you."

But when I burst through the door from the private suites to the common room, I stopped. Through the darkness, I spotted a figure creeping up the stairs. I quickly flicked the nearest light switch, which bathed the person in a faint light. They froze.

"Saffron?" I asked into the dimness. "Is that you?"

"Oh, um, hi Poppy."

"What are you doing? It's the middle of the night. Did you go outside? Is everything okay?"

"Everything's fine. I just popped out for a second to get some fresh air, that's all." Saffron let out a single halfhearted giggle. "Must be wedding jitters."

I tightened my robe. "Did you see a cat out there?"

"A cat? No, why?"

I shook my head. "No reason. I don't want to keep you. Sleep well."

"Goodnight."

Saffron ascended the stairs out of sight and I returned to Greta's snores. Before I shut the door behind me, a scream peeled through the house and my stomach dropped.

Greta shot up in bed. "That wasn't the alarm."

"No, it definitely wasn't."

I rushed to the common room to find Saffron hurrying down the stairwell.

"Charmaine, Charmaine," she wailed. "She needs help!"

I followed Saffron up the stairs and ran into the other six women slowly emerging from their respective suites. Through the open doorway to her room, we spotted Charmaine laying limply on the floor. Her left leg bent sharply under her body. Harsh, red marks scuffed her bare ivory neck, and a spilled Klover Kombucha bottle lay nearby.

Scanning the group, I spotted Maya. "Maya, can you help?"

Maya stared at me, shocked and dazed. "Oh, right." She rushed forward and knelt beside Charmaine as I corralled the others out of the room to give her space. She picked up the woman's wrist then lay it by her side after a moment. She reached for Charmaine's neck, and felt there too, then leaned forward, listening at the woman's mouth.

While I held the ladies back with my outstretched hands, Maya started chest compressions, working on the woman between feeling for a pulse. A few agonizing minutes later, she stopped and shook her head with a sob. "She's gone."

Three

DEPUTY TODD NEWMAN, lean and lanky, tapped a pen against his clipboard as the last of the emergency personnel left the house. He wore his oversized, wide-brimmed hat proudly, and it cast a menacing shadow across his face.

I clutched at my robe, huddled next to Greta and Lily in the common room, and the commune women wept in a tight-knit circle nearby. Jennifer, always the outsider, sat in the same wingback chair she'd occupied the previous day.

"Well, well, well, Miss Lewis," Deputy Todd drawled. "Another body turns up in your vicinity, heinously murdered, and I'm woken up once again in the dark of night. Wish I could say I'm shocked, but that ship has sailed."

My lip stiffened. "And I wish that, *once again*, a murderer hadn't slipped through under your nose. Aren't you supposed to protect this community?"

He bristled.

"What about Charmaine?" Saffron blubbered her words through tears.

"The coroner will take care of her," Deputy Todd said. "In the meantime, I'll want to have a little chat with each and every one of you." He pointed at the gaggle of bridesmaids.

Greta and Lily shuffled as if to retreat to their rooms, but Deputy Todd stopped them.

"And you three," he said. "I'm going to want statements from all of you." He tapped his pen against the clipboard again, then in a grumbly voice said, "Especially you, Miss Lewis."

"We're not skipping town, if that's what you're afraid of." I waved Greta and Lily to return to their rooms and stayed behind in the common room.

Deputy Todd didn't answer. Instead, he turned to the huddled women. "I want to start with the one who found the body. Who's that?"

Saffron let out an agonizing wail. "That's me."

I walked over to the sobbing woman. "Don't worry, Saffron. I'll stay with you."

"The rest of you remain here." Deputy Todd's boney finger lingered accusingly on the group, then he waved Saffron and me into the kitchen, away from the others.

I eased Saffron into the chair by the small kitchen table.

"Now," Deputy Todd began, "tell me what happened. Tell me everything."

Saffron nodded with a sniffle. "I... I went upstairs and opened the door to the room Charmaine and I shared. I assumed she was awake since the light was on, but then I saw her on the floor and..." She trailed off with another heaving wail and buried her face in her hands.

Deputy Todd scribbled a notation on his clipboard. "Were there any witnesses to your discovery of the victim's body?"

"Well, I... You see, it was dark when I came back, and..." She glanced at me, then back to the deputy. "Poppy saw me."

Caught off guard, I choked on my words. "I, uh..."

"Just where exactly were you returning from?" Deputy Todd asked.

"I'd only stepped outside for a minute. To get some air. Nerves. Wedding jitters, that kind of thing. I thought Charmaine would be asleep, so I tried to be quiet."

Deputy Todd grunted and scrawled on his clipboard before underlining it with two harsh swooshes. He peered up at me from under the brim of his oversized hat. "These women are sharing certain rooms, is that correct, Miss Lewis?"

I nodded. "Yes. Saffron and Charmaine had the largest room—the one with the large Victorian furniture. Kismet and Jennifer are sharing. Clover and Ziggy have another room." I pinched at the spot between my eyes, trying to keep it straight. "And Maya and Heavenleigh are sharing the last room."

Deputy Todd scribbled furiously. "Mm-hmm. I think I want a few words alone. If you'll excuse us." He eyed the swivel door behind me and bobbed his head once toward it.

I shared a last look with Saffron, squeezed her shoulder for support, then left her to Deputy Todd's interrogation.

Thus, the early morning hours waned on, as each

woman gave her statement and slowly shuffled upstairs to bed. I served as the go-between, waking each as her time came until only I remained to be questioned.

"Interesting stories," Deputy Todd said as I finally took my seat at the kitchen table. "What about yours?"

"Everyone went to their rooms around eleven o'clock and I went to bed too. It had been a long day. I'd had a new security system installed and Greta and Lily didn't like my new toaster, and—"

"Get back to the murder, Miss Lewis."

"Right. We all went to bed, then I got up because Mayor Dewey kept tripping my door alarm. The last time I got up I saw Saffron inching up the stairs. She said she'd needed some air, so I said goodnight and then a minute or so later she screamed. That's when I ran upstairs and saw Charmaine's body."

"Mm-hmm." Scribble.

I set my elbow on the table and let the weight of my head and drooping eyelids fall against my palm.

Deputy Todd stopped scribbling. "Oh, I'm sorry, Miss Lewis. Are you tired? Well, gee golly, I hate to pull you out of your nice warm bed and take up your precious time with this pesky murder investigation."

I sat up straight, but my eyelids continued to droop.

"Anything else you can remember?"

I blinked through tired eyes. "At this hour? No."

"Fine." The chair made an awful screech as Deputy Todd scooted it back from the table. "I'm sure I don't have to remind you, but this is now a law enforcement matter. No poking around or asking questions, got it?"

My voice got three shades sweeter. "I'm sure I don't know what you mean."

"Don't play games with me, Miss Lewis." He pointed his forefinger and middle finger at his eyes, then swiveled them my way. "I've got my eyes on you. No funny business."

I hid my eye roll behind an exhausted droop.

When I finally showed him to the door, he stepped out onto the porch, then turned to face me and hefted his pants by the belt. "Remember, Miss Lewis, leave this one to the big guns."

"I assure you I have no intention of poking around in your investigation."

He grunted as the door closed in his face, and I stared at the spot his smug mug had just been. I had *every* intention of poking around in his investigation.

***

The next morning, I peeked through the swivel door into the dining room from the kitchen. Saffron sat silently in her chair at the big dining table, eyes downcast, while others talked in hushed tones with their neighbors, no doubt discussing last night's events. Ziggy and Jennifer were absent, and I'd seen neither of them all morning.

I let the door ease closed. "This one's going to be rough."

"Yup." Greta worked at the stove, preparing delicate crepes with a deceptively deft hand. A quick swirl of the spreader left a perfect circle of batter in the center of the pan.

Although gruff, my housekeeper and chef could make magic in the kitchen. I bit my lip and glanced around at the smart devices I'd had installed in what was essentially Greta's domain. The toaster, the coffeemaker.

She'd kept a wide berth since the previous day. I felt a pang of regret at replacing the appliances with versions she would never utilize, but it was time to step into the modern day.

"I've already called the Smarty Pants technician. He'll be by sometime today to check on the appliances."

"Don't forget the sensitivity on that front door alarm. Felt like an obscure Russian torture tactic, slowly melting your mind until you're nothing but a husk of yourself."

"I've already turned off some of the default settings so it shouldn't go off as much. We're all low on sleep. Let's just get through the day, starting with breakfast."

"This is the last one." She folded the thin pancake in one smooth motion and transferred it to a nearby platter.

I took it up in two hands and steeled myself as I swung through the door into the dining room. "I hope you all like crepes."

They each started at my entrance and the chatting died down.

I set breakfast on the table just as the blaring front door alert sounded from the phone in my pocket. Suppressing a cringe, I turned it off as Jennifer tread lightly into the dining room and slipped into an empty chair.

"Where have you been all morning?" Kismet asked her.

"I went for a walk outside. The air off the ocean smells wonderful this early."

Clover picked up the fork by her plate and fiddled with it between her fingers. "Should we really be having breakfast at a time like this?"

"What else are we supposed to do?" Kismet asked. "We've got to eat." She leaned across the table and spoke pointedly to Clover. "Is something on your mind making you lose your appetite?"

Clover dropped the fork. "I've got nothing to hide. You of all people shouldn't be throwing accusations around."

Kismet flinched.

Heavenleigh spoke up. "I've got nothing to hide either. Charmaine and I were on good terms, but it sounds like that wasn't the case with the rest of you."

"Now hold on a second," Maya said.

At the same time, Kismet asked, "What are you suggesting?"

And over them both, Jennifer piped up with, "I'd barely just met the woman."

The crepes sat untouched at the center of the table. It appeared no one had much of an appetite.

"Can I get anyone anything else?" I tried to keep my voice calm and uplifting. The back-and-forth had become heated, and diffusing the tension seemed necessary, although it wasn't lost on me that most of the women appeared more defensive than mournful.

Saffron, who until now had sat morosely silent at the head of the table, let out a heavy sigh. "Could we all stop fighting, please? None of it will bring Charmaine back."

The women fell silent.

"We're all here, together. Despite our loss, I want us to continue. I want to continue with the wedding."

Maya bolted upright in her chair. "Saffron, you're in shock. We all are. I don't know if this is the best time for—"

Saffron held up a hand to stop her. "I've given this a lot of thought. Everything is already set and I can't let

Chad down. I... I want to try to make this a happy memory. Papa Zamora always said, 'When lost in the darkness...'"

The other commune girls finished in unison. "'Be the spark of light.'"

Kismet patted the bride's hand. "We'll make it special for you."

Saffron took Kismet's hand in hers. "Kizzy, my best, best friend, I know it's a lot to ask, but would you take over as Maid of Honor?"

The woman's eyes watered and a twinge at the corner of her mouth held back a smile. "Of course. I'd be honored."

"Matron of Honor, you mean," Clover said. "She's married, remember?"

Kismet shot Clover a glare. "I can be whatever I want."

"It's all right," Saffron said. "We don't need to be so formal."

"If we're going forward with this," Maya began, "I'd suggest we dedicate time to release our negative energy and replace it with a positive, uplifting force."

Heavenleigh nodded enthusiastically. "An energy reset is exactly what we need."

Maya caught my eye. "Poppy, do you know a place where we can set up for a yoga class? Your house is big, but we'll want somewhere we can really spread out."

"I think the Starry Cove community center is available tomorrow morning. I can check with the mayor."

"Perfect," Maya said. "That gives us a few days to focus on our mental and physical wellbeing before the wedding." Maya looked at each woman in turn. "Doctor's orders."

***

With breakfast done and everything washed up, I set Greta to servicing the rooms while I headed out the door to visit my friend's bakery. With any luck, a hot gooey cinnamon roll would be waiting with my name on it.

Instead, I entered into a flurry of floury action. Angie Owens, the best baker in Vista County, scurried red-faced from the display case around the counter and through the entry into the back kitchen.

In a departure from our usual morning routine, Harper Tillman, still in her mail-carrier uniform, wiped down the counter with broad strokes of her long, spindly arms. With each sweep, the tight curls on her head threatened to escape the rainbow headband she always wore.

"Poppy, good." Harper stopped just long enough to toss a tea towel my way. "Grab this and help me clean everything off."

"What's going on?"

"Angie's in a spiral because Cesar's out and she and Shelby are working on a menu for a wedding and the bride and groom are about to show up for cake tasting."

"Saffron's coming here?"

"Who?" Harper didn't look up from her furious scrubbing.

I joined her at the counter and started my own wipe down. "The bride."

Harper stopped. "Don't tell me Lovie's gossip was true."

Unsurprisingly, Lovie Newman, our deputy sheriff's chin-wagging wife, had already spread news of the murder through town.

"I'm afraid so. It was awful."

Angie emerged from the kitchen carrying a towering stack of bright white plates. "What's awful?"

"There really *was* a murder at Poppy's place last night."

The plates clattered as Angie dumped the stack onto the counter. They wobbled precariously, but Angie only had her eyes on me. "Oh no. I thought Lovie was just toying with us." She toddled to my side and wrapped her pudgy arms around me. "I'm so sorry. Are you okay?"

"She'd better be," Harper said. "With as many murders as she's seen, I'd bet—"

Angie's glare cut Harper off, then she turned back to me. "Let me get you a cinnamon roll and some coffee. You sit right there and I'll take care of you."

"What about me?" Harper asked, flinging the towel onto the floury countertop. "Don't I get any sugar?"

"You already had some. Now, get back to work."

"I don't even work here," Harper said through a grumble. But she retrieved the towel and resumed her wipe down.

I took a seat at the sole table in the bakery and dove into a fork-full of the hot cinnamon roll Angie placed in front of me. Angie's bakery wasn't a place for the locals to hang out—although the three of us did quite frequently. Instead, a steady stream of customers popped in and popped right back out with their purchases. No need to linger since Shelby Shepard's diner was right next door and you could get bottomless coffee there.

But I liked that the bakery had just enough seating for us. It meant we could talk freely with no chance of being overheard.

"Harper said the bride and groom are coming in for cake tasting. The bride is staying at my place with a bunch of her bridesmaids. Minus one."

Angie, back at the tower of plates, began to skate them across the cleaned portions of the counter in a row. "Yes, and they could be here any minute and I'm not ready because Roy is out of town again and Cesar is on vacation and I was supposed to have some additional help for this wedding but all three of my caterers flaked and now it's just me and Shelby and we can't do it alone because we've got the rest of the wedding food to prepare and I don't know who's even going to serve the food now that we're short-staffed so I guess I'm under a bit of pressure right now." The final plate spun to a stop.

"Maybe you should sit down, Angie," Harper said. "Take a breather. Meditate."

I bolted upright in my chair. "Oh, that reminds me I wanted to ask you a question, Harper."

She looked at me with a dramatically raised eyebrow. Harper was always suspicious of requests.

"One of my guests wants to use the community center tomorrow. She's putting on a yoga class."

Harper waved her towel with a flick of her wrist. "No problem, it's free. Mayor Dewey's been spending his time with that Daisy, anyway. Oof!" Her nose wrinkled. "She's an ugly one."

"They've been running around like a gang," Angie said. "Shelby said they tried to sneak into the diner's kitchen through the backdoor. They almost made off with a chicken fried steak."

I remembered the shadowy figures I'd spotted

through the sidelights the previous night. "They were snooping around my house, too."

"Think of them like security guards," Harper said. "You've got a cat to catch mice and rats and a dog to growl at peeping toms."

Angie giggled. "Daisy doesn't growl. She screeches like a prepubescent boy."

"Her looks will scare off any prowlers then," Harper said. "They'd never expect to run into a hairless, toothless mutt shrieking at them like a banshee."

"She's got teeth," I said. "Those two little snaggled fangs in the front, and she still has a few tufts of hair on her head. But I don't care what they do as long as she doesn't scare my guests." I picked at the cinnamon roll crumbs left on my plate. "I might join that yoga class tomorrow. Angie, you should too. Calm some of those nerves of yours."

"What nerves?"

"Charlie likes yoga," Harper said. "Can I tell her about it?"

I shrugged. I'd already invited Harper and Angie, so there was no reason to snub Harper's crush. "I don't think Maya would mind. She's pretty laid back for a doctor. But they all grew up on a commune, so I guess that was instilled at a young age."

Angie scooted down the line of plates, plopping a different cake sample onto each one as she went. "I don't think I can make the time for it. I've got so much to do, and without those caterers to help…"

I caught Harper's eye, and she flinched, then she mouthed *No* while shaking her head.

"Harper and I can help."

Harper groaned.

Angie lit up. "Really?"

"Of course."

Angie tapped her chin. "In that case, can we have a quick meeting at your place tonight? I want to get everyone on the same page. Weddings can be tricky, and we have the rehearsal dinner to cater as well."

"Sure. And I know two others who have enough free time to help with the catering, too."

Harper pressed her hands together in prayer. "Don't say Greta and Lily. Please don't say Greta and Lily."

"Greta and Lily."

***

The bakery's doorbell jingled as Saffron and a tall, yet unremarkable man entered.

"Welcome," Angie said in a cheery voice. "You must be Saffron and Chad. I'm Angie Owens. Everything is almost set up." Angie shooed Harper from behind the counter and began to adjust the various cake plates, although they already looked straight to me.

Saffron spotted me, placed her arm in Chad's, then approached me at the small table. "Poppy, this is my fiancé, Chad."

He was a wave of bland beigeness, with the same bland oatmeal hair as his sister. He wore his taupe polo shirt buttoned to the tippy-top, clean and proper. I probably couldn't pick him out in a crowd. He seemed the exact opposite of airy-fairy Saffron, who flitted with each step like a butterfly and let her blonde hair flow freely.

"Nice to meet you, Chad."

He only nodded in response. A man of few words,

apparently.

"Chad and I would be so happy if you would attend our wedding. You've been so hospitable."

My eyebrows rose slightly. I'd just agreed to help with the catering, but how could I say no? I was sure I could squeeze it in. "I'd love to, thank you for the invitation."

"Of course, and you can bring your friends, too. I want this to be a welcoming ceremony."

"How lovely," I said, genuinely touched, "but I have to ask, are you feeling up for this cake tasting after last night?"

Saffron patted Chad on the arm and turned him toward the cake counter. "Why don't you go see which cakes look best. I'll be over in a minute." Once he'd left, she took the seat across from me. "It's not easy. I'll admit. But everyone is already here, and the whole thing is planned and put together. I don't want to let anyone down."

"Kismet seems pleased with her new role."

Saffron broke her eyes away from mine. "Kismet is my best, best friend, but she can be very petty sometimes."

"I guess that's what I don't understand. If Kismet is your best friend, then why was Charmaine your Maid of Honor?"

"Oh," Saffron said, trailing off. She twirled a finger around a loose lock of her blonde hair. "I guess I was sort of torn between friends."

I cocked my head. "Kismet seemed pretty disappointed."

Saffron winced and let out a heavy sigh. "Okay, there's something else." Her eyes shifted to Chad. He chatted with Angie at the cake counter, well out of earshot. "Kismet was causing problems. Love her to death, but there'd been some drama between her and Charmaine."

"Color me surprised."

"I know," Saffron said with a slight eye roll. "But this was real drama. You see, Kismet's husband, Barry, is Chad's best man."

"Wouldn't Kismet be the obvious choice then?"

"Not exactly. They sort of aren't talking."

"Kismet and Barry?"

"Uh-huh. So Chad begged me not to choose Kismet. I wanted to, I really did because she truly is my best friend in the whole wide world, but I did it for him."

"Why aren't Kismet and Barry talking?"

Saffron curled a bit of hair between her fingers. "Um, well, Charmaine and Barry *may* have been having an affair."

I blinked in surprise. "An affair?" My imagination went in a hundred directions, but they all ended with Kismet having a pretty darn good motive for offing Charmaine.

"It's over now. But it made things a bit awkward for a while. No one else knows, so don't say anything, okay? Kizzy would absolutely rage if she knew I'd told you."

"And now? You asked Kismet to be your Maid of Honor this morning."

Another glance at Chad. "I haven't told him about that *quite* yet. But I figured since Charmaine...you know, that Kismet and Barry could work it out."

"Don't you think that looks a little suspicious? That the woman her husband was cheating with is killed and now Kismet takes her place as Maid of Honor?"

Saffron bit her lip. "Gosh. I never really saw it that way. Kizzy would never do anything like that."

"And wouldn't pairing Charmaine with Barry be like pouring salt on the wound?"

This time Saffron suddenly appeared keenly interested in her fingernails. "It's complicated. Plus, I don't want to bore you with all our little dramas. I want to make sure everyone has a good time and enjoys the festivities, so let's forget about it, okay?" She gave me a little tap on the shoulder as if to seal the deal.

"Honey," Chad called from the counter, "she's ready to start."

"Gotta go," Saffron said with a smile. "Thanks for chatting." She took one step, then turned back. With a pleading look, she added, "And please don't say anything about the affair."

As Saffron took her seat at the counter, I was swirling with thoughts of Kismet's multiple motives. It was almost too much, too obvious. Or was it?

***

I left the bakery with a lot on my mind, but that was all wiped away as soon as I stepped through the door. Jennifer stood on the sidewalk speaking with two equally beige people, dull and unimaginative in appearance like generic paper dolls, who I surmised were her parents. Another figure joined them. Our town gossip, Lovie Newman, immersed and thriving in her element. But they weren't who made me stop in my tracks. That was the other woman with them, a woman who reminded me of a blonde-bobbed snake with red glasses—Veronica Valentine, journalist-in-name-only from the Vista View newspaper.

I quickly pivoted to walk the other way, but I'd been spotted.

"Poppy Lewis," Veronica called. "Would you like to make a statement?"

"No, thank you."

"I'm *so* shocked to hear what happened," Lovie said to me. "I can't believe yet *another* death at your house. It must be awful."

The beige woman spoke up, nose pointed in the air, "I'm not entirely surprised that something so scandalous would happen involving Saffron."

"What a troubled young lady," Lovie said, nodding along with Jennifer's mother. "You're both so understanding to let this marriage go on, what with the death of the Maid of Honor."

"Saffron insisted," Mother Beige said. "We tried to talk Chad out of it once we found out, but he wouldn't listen. He's wrapped entirely around that woman's finger."

Jennifer crossed her arms and rubbed them as if chilled. "I'm still struggling to get the image of that woman lying there, white-faced, with nothing but a kombucha bottle nearby. What a horrible way to die."

"Well," Lovie said with a huff, "the timing is just terrible. Not only are all these lovely wedding guests in town, but we've just had a new resident take over ownership of our bookstore. What a way to welcome him to town." She tsked and shook her head dramatically. "I'll have to be sure to bring him a welcome present. It's important to counteract any negative impressions right away. Poppy, you should introduce yourself and apologize, especially since this happened at your property. You know, head off any damage it may cause."

I wanted to tell her to mind her own business, but that would be like telling a dog not to sniff your neighbor's butt. "I'll swing by and say hello."

As I stepped away to take my leave, Veronica popped up by my side, the clack of her heels piercing the pavement in lock step.

"I'll give you one more chance to make a statement, Poppy. The article runs tomorrow."

"Get lost, Veronica."

"Is that a no? Not a single statement about last night's events at your establishment? Another murder under your roof. Repeat violent crimes on your watch?"

I screeched to a halt. "Actually, that would be Deputy Todd Newman's watch."

Her eyes gleamed. "You're suggesting this was law enforcement's incompetence?" She thrust her recorder into my face, waiting for me to say more.

I ground my teeth. Should have kept my mouth shut. "No comment," I said.

Veronica pulled the recorder back and spoke into it directly. "Poppy Lewis, proprietress of the Pearl-by-the-Sea bed-and-breakfast in Starry Cove, had no comment when asked about the multiple murders at her business other than to suggest that law enforcement's diligence may have been lacking."

I pursed my lips. "Stop trying to bait me, Veronica. I have nothing to say to you."

"Would you like to correct anything *on the record*?" Veronica smirked and held her recorder to me once again.

"No comment," I said through gritted teeth.

Her eyes flashed. "Feeling guilty about something?"

"No comment."

"Feeling a twinge of blame, perhaps?"

"No—"

My words dropped at the sight of a woman making her way down the street. It wasn't difficult to tell that it was Clover—the head-to-toe crimson Klover Kombucha outfit gave her away. She shuffled along the far sidewalk struggling with a heavy crate of kombucha balanced in her arms. When she reached Shelby's Diner, she tugged open the door with the tip of her foot and slipped inside.

"No what?" Veronica practically shoved her recorder up my nose.

I pulled my eyes from where Clover had disappeared and turned to the reporter. "No comment, Veronica. Ever."

Four

WITH VERONICA IN my dust, I entered the diner a moment after Clover. She'd already managed to snag Shelby Shepard's attention and was speaking energetically to the diner's owner over the box of kombucha perched on the counter.

Shelby held up her palm. "I'm going to stop you there, dearie. I don't even know what kombookie is."

"Kombucha," Clover corrected. "It's an organic fermented tea beverage. An alternative to sugary sodas or bland regular tea. Your customers are going to love it."

"Fermented?" Shelby waved her hands and took one step backward, her towering beehive wobbling like gelatine. "My liquor license is already one fake I.D. away from oblivion, dearie."

Clover leaned farther over the counter, making up the distance. "It's technically considered non-alcoholic. Klover Kombucha has an alcohol content of less than half a percent. It comes in a variety of flavors." She rustled through the bottles and pulled one out. "This one's called

Kokonut, and there's also an energy drink version we call Kickstart. They're refreshing and delicious. Here, try it." Clover shoved the Kokonut bottle toward Shelby, but she backed up against the wall behind the slim counter.

Once she spotted me, Shelby's eyes widened, and I read her unspoken plea for help. "Hi Clover," I said. "Are you selling your kombucha?"

Clover turned to me and I flinched. Her teeth gleamed through a rigid smile and her eyes were wide and unblinking. "Sure am. Klover Kombucha is the perfect beverage to fill your fridge."

"You might want to tone down the sales pitch," I said. "This is a pretty small town, and most aren't used to such a hard push."

Clover's plastic face softened. She spared a glance at Shelby, who was still pressed against the wall. "Right. Sorry." She gave Shelby an apologetic smile.

Freed from Clover's aggressive tactics, Shelby scurried into the back kitchen.

"You're tenacious," I said. "I'll give you that."

She sighed heavily and leaned against the crate of kombucha. "I'm nice. I smile. The product is great. I thought it would sell itself. I guess I thought all of this would be easier. This sales part."

"Things aren't going so hot, then?"

She slumped into the first bar stool at the counter. "Abysmal."

I eased onto the stool next to her. "Charmaine mentioned a board meeting. Was she your business partner?"

"Business partner." Clover repeated my words with scorn. "You could call her that. She was supposed to be a *silent* partner, but somehow her voice managed to pop up more and more, less and less silent." Her fingers tapped at the cap of one of the bottles. *Tap, tap.*

"The kombucha must be pretty good. She seemed to like it."

"That's an understatement." *Tap, tap, tap.* "She could have single-handedly guzzled away all our product."

I chose my next words carefully. "There was even a bottle next to her last night."

The tapping stopped. "No surprise. Like I said, Charmaine loved the stuff."

"I'm so sorry about Charmaine," I said. "You all seem so close. It must be hard."

Clover gave me an appraising look as if determining if I were being genuine or not. "Yeah, we're close. When you grow up like we did you tend to group together, whether you're similar or not. There weren't a lot of options, so you're sort of forced into friendship for better or for worse."

"I can't believe any of you would want to hurt each other then."

Clover scoffed. "Oh, don't be fooled into thinking that. We could scuffle with the best of them. Charmaine, in particular, would goad you until you fought back. But she aways managed to escape consequence." *Tap, tap, tap.* "I think she was one of Papa Zamora's favorites."

"That's the commune leader?"

"Yeah, and he's also Heavenleigh's dad. So, I guess Heavenleigh was the real favorite." Clover said this last part with a sarcastic chuckle.

"Sounds like Charmaine got away with a lot."

"Yep." *Tap, tap, tap.*

"And the others? How did they react to Charmaine's death?"

Clover shrugged. "Probably the same way I did. Shock. Disbelief. Surprisingly not as sad as I thought I'd be. I don't want to sound callous, but like I said we were more friends by necessity and obligation."

"So then, who do you think could have done this? It's pretty bold."

Clover shrugged again. "No idea. I spent the night in my room and didn't hear or see anything until I heard Saffron screaming."

"What about Ziggy? You two shared a room."

She chewed at her bottom lip and took a moment to respond. "Ziggy left at some point. She'd had too much to drink. You saw that at least. She was practically stumbling over herself all night. I think she needed to, you know, let it out."

"Gotcha. But you aren't sure where she went?"

"I just assumed she went to the bathroom. She didn't even make it to breakfast this morning. Still sleeping off whatever hangover was left."

"Makes sense." I went silent, mulling this over in my head. Finally, I asked, "Was Ziggy goaded by Charmaine like you were?"

Clover practically choked. "Goaded? She wasn't just goaded she was bullied up a wall by Charmaine. She definitely got it the worst." She shook her head at some memory. "We were all so surprised at how she turned up yesterday. Looks totally different. She used to be so mousy and quiet. She's like night and day now."

"Was it just me," I said, "or did she look a bit like Charmaine?"

"Yes," Clover said in quick agreement. "I thought so, too. I didn't ask her, of course. Besides, by the time I could ask her in private she was so loopy she probably wouldn't have understood a word of it. She just sort of stumbled onto her bed at that point."

"I'm sure she'll be fine once she gets some rest."

"I hope so." Clover hopped off the stool. "I've got to keep pushing these."

"You should try Ursula's general store. That's where most of us grab stuff if we don't want to drive all the way to the grocery store in Vista."

"And where's this general store?"

"C'mon," I said, "I'll show you. I've got someone there I need to talk to, anyway."

I opened the door and let Clover through with her heavy load. She'd mentioned that Ziggy left their room, and that Ziggy had reason to dislike, or even hate, Charmaine. But could a stumbling drunk really overtake a grown woman in a fight? Maybe if she was driven enough, motivated enough. Maybe if there was enough on the line.

***

"Good morning." I waved to an older woman with unnaturally bright red hair who stood behind the counter. I held the door open as Clover and her kombucha toddled through.

"What's this?" Ursula asked with a gesture to Clover.

"It's your lucky day," Clover replied. "Have I got a deal for you."

I left Clover to shill her wares and made my way to a tiny alcove in the back of the general store that housed the town's pharmacy. At the pharmacy's counter, Ryan MacKenzie, with his tidy, sandy brown hair, glasses, and periwinkle cardigan focused all of his attention on counting pills into a small bottle. He only looked up once I tapped on the plexiglass.

"Well, hello there." His roguish Scottish accent belied his gentle features. "And how may I help such a beautiful woman?"

"Do you want to go on a date?"

His left eyebrow rose under the rimless edge of his glasses. "That depends on what kind of date. Are we talking flowers and a restaurant that has three little dollar signs next to its name online or a place with one dollar sign and no dress code?"

"Don't play," I said. "You'd say yes to either."

He smiled. "For you, anything."

Ryan, the town's pharmacist, was also my boyfriend, and with every unconscious adjustment of his glasses he made my heart flutter.

"Based on your playful mood," he said, "I'll assume Lovie's rumors aren't true."

"What rumors?"

"That there was a murder at the Pearl last night."

The smile I'd been wearing dropped. "Ah. Unfortunately, that bit is true. I've got a bridal party staying, and it was the Maid of Honor. We had a doctor at the house, but it wasn't enough to save the woman."

"Are you all right?"

"Me?" I asked in surprise. "I'm fine. The others..." I glanced at Clover, who was shaking a bottle of kombucha in Ursula's face. "They seem mostly unaffected so far. I don't think they liked the woman very much."

Ryan cleared his throat. "I take it Deputy Todd is on the case and actively investigating?"

I rolled my eyes from Clover back to Ryan. "What are you suggesting?"

"Nothing, nothing. What was this about a date?"

"The wedding," I said. "The bride invited me. I promised Angie I'd work the catering crew, but I can still attend the ceremony. There'll be a free meal and one of Angie's cakes in it for you."

"Black-tie?"

"No, but something nice. Don't go overboard."

He nodded. "So, no kilt?" Even with his head down, I could see the smirk at the corner of his mouth.

"I wouldn't say no to the kilt."

"All right. It's a date, then."

"I've got another question," I said. "How's Daisy's training going? She's been cruising the town with Mayor Dewey and I think he may be a bad influence. They were creeping around my porch all last night."

"Aye. Quite the gang, those two. I'll mention it to Ethan. She's his responsibility, remember?"

"Right. 'Responsibility will build character.' Those were your exact words."

The door to the general store clanked open and Kismet entered. She peered around, spotted me and waved, then continued down an aisle before disappearing from my view.

"That one." I nodded toward Kismet. "She's the *new* Maid of Honor."

"And I'm sure Deputy Todd has made note of that," Ryan said.

"Huh? Oh, right. I'm sure he's all over it." I took a

few steps away from the pharmacy counter and gave Ryan a quick wave. "I'll talk to you more later. Keep that kilt handy."

I dipped down the aisle where Kismet had disappeared and found her bent overlooking at the options for dental floss. "Can I help you find something? I know the layout of this store by heart."

She snatched a package from the shelf and rose from her crouch. "No need. Found it."

"I suppose I should congratulate you," I said.

"For what?"

"For being selected as Maid of Honor."

Kismet stared at me stone-faced. "It's hardly an honor to be second best."

"Still, Saffron didn't hesitate to ask you this morning."

"Honestly, I don't really care."

I placed myself strategically in the center of the aisle which blocked Kismet's escape. Not that I was trying to hold her there, but I wanted to get my questions out before she could scurry away.

Kismet's eyes checked over my shoulder. Clover still had Ursula locked into her sales pitch.

"It's odd, though, that Saffron called you her best friend, but didn't choose you initially."

Kismet continued to show no reaction. "Is it?"

"It's okay if you're disappointed," I said. "I would be, too."

"I couldn't tell you why she chose Charmaine, okay? I feel like I hardly know Saffron anymore. She's been so wrapped up in wedding planning and guests and—" Her eyes narrowed the faintest bit. "Why do you care?"

"Me?" I asked in feigned surprise. "I'm just curious. I get such interesting guests all the time and I suppose I get swirled into their stories."

"Well, there's no story here," Kismet said, "just a back-up Maid of Honor."

"You shouldn't look at it that way."

"Why not?" she asked sharply. "Saffron's got the nerve to ask Charmaine, *of all people*, then beg me to step in when that didn't work out."

"If it makes you feel any better, Saffron told me she felt torn between the two of you, so I don't think the choice was easy for her."

"It shouldn't have been hard at all. Charmaine is—" She cut off before finishing, shaking her head instead. "She wasn't a good person."

"I'm starting to get that. It's no surprise someone would want to harm her then, right?"

Kismet shifted on her feet. "I guess."

"Maybe someone who had a lot of beef with her? Someone who was betrayed?"

Kismet's face was stone again.

Saffron had asked me not to say anything, but I had to tease out this lead. "Saffron told me about the affair," I said.

Kismet's jaw hardened.

"Trust me when I say, that must be really hard to get over. If there's someone you want to commiserate with, I'm—"

"I'm already over it. And Saffron should mind her own business instead of talking about other people. She's great at spilling other peoples' secrets but wants us to keep hers?" Kismet scoffed. "Typical."

I leaned in. "What secrets?"

Kismet fell silent, but her lips scrunched as though trying to keep something in. Finally, she asked, "Did she tell you why she was sneaking out last night?"

"To get fresh air?" I asked hopefully.

"She was sneaking out to the woods. Some super-secret ritual or something. Crystals and sage and candles and all that. *Very* Saffron."

A secret ritual? "What kind of ritual?"

"You'll have to ask her."

"Why do you think she'd lie to me?"

Kismet shrugged, her shoulders dipping up and down in a dramatic fashion. "You'd have to ask her. Maybe then she'll understand how it feels to have *her* secrets spilled all over town."

"I don't think she meant any harm," I said.

Her phone rang and Kismet checked the screen. I caught a glimpse at the name—Gardener—before it disappeared back into her pocket.

A faint smile had touched her lips, but it faded when she looked up at me again. "Maybe she was conducting a death wish spell on Charmaine. Maybe she wasn't gone at all and was just creating an alibi. She's clearly not who I thought she was."

Kismet bumped my shoulder as she pushed past me and headed toward the checkout to make her purchase, leaving me to wonder what Saffron was really up to that previous night.

Five

PASTOR BASIL MEYERS stood by the picket fence that lined the property of the Fellowship of the Faith church. He waved emphatically to catch my attention, the sleeves of his woolen cardigan flapping in the wind.

I made my way along the sidewalk toward the church and came upon the bookstore. Lovie had mentioned there was a new owner, but the windows were taped over with brown paper and the door was locked. I checked along the outer windows and noticed the paper had peeled up in one small corner.

My head whipped up and down the street, checking for Lovie or Deputy Todd who would take my snooping the wrong way. Not that I *was* snooping—I'd been asked to greet the new owner, after all. As discreetly as I could, I knelt down and peered into the darkened bookstore.

With my face squished against the window, whatever faint daylight may have illuminated the space was now blocked. Without clear lighting, there wasn't much to see. A single dust mote floated by, but otherwise, there was no other movement. Definitely nobody home.

"Anyone there?" Pastor Basil called from across the road.

I jogged over. "Nope. Empty. Lovie said there was a new owner, but it looks shut up pretty tight."

The pastor adjusted his round glasses. "There's definitely someone new, but I haven't seen much of him. Cruises in and behind that door without as much as a 'hey man.'"

"Well, he's not there now. Do you know his name?"

"Like I said, man, he's on the skiff. Maybe he's not down with the church?"

"I'm sure he's not dodging you, probably just busy getting the place ready to open."

"I heard about Charmaine. Sad days, Poppy." He shook his head woefully.

"I'm so sorry. I know the girls were looking forward to seeing you again."

Pastor Basil looked back at the cobblestone church, quaint and surrounded by flowerbeds to which he lovingly tended. "Saffron said she knew that she wanted me to officiate." He dabbed at a tear that had sprung up in the corner of his eye. "Sweet flower, that Saffron. All those kids. It's a real tragedy, man. Real tragedy."

I wrapped an arm around the pastor, remembering that even those who uplift us in our time of need require comforting themselves sometimes.

"I wish I'd been able to see her one last time." He tipped up his glasses and wiped away tears on one scratchy sleeve of his sweater. "Just glad I can be here for the others."

"I'm sure they're glad to have you nearby, too. What

do you remember about her? Charmaine. The other girls, too. They all seem so interesting, and growing up on a commune must have been a unique experience."

"Unique? I don't know about that. We were just living in peace and free love. Emphasis on the free love, ya dig? It was a groovy time. Blurred lines, all that."

"And they were close?"

"Close as could be. Charmaine, though, she was precocious. A mite little troublemaker, too, man. Real observant, real sharp."

"But she got along with all the girls?"

"Well, now, I wouldn't say they always got along. Ziggy, she was a tiny thing and Charmaine would just roll right over her. It's good to see that they're all still friends now." His voice cracked and tears began to well again. "They'll be here for the rehearsal tomorrow. Walk through the church, that kind of thing."

I stared up at the church, its cobblestone sides bare. "It looks so exposed now that Ethan's cleared up all the ivy."

"It'll grow back," he said, casting a look at the cobbled wall. "No worries, Poppy. That ivy grows like weed. It'll be covered back over in no time."

No time couldn't come soon enough. Even here at this angle I could make out the faint pattern in the cobblestone wall. That same pattern from Claude Goodwin's secret map supposedly marked the spot of his hidden treasure. Now, I needed to find out where on the grounds it was hidden. Doctor Everett Goodwin, leader of a shadowy group known as the Gold Hand, had shown himself, and I knew he wasn't going to rest until he got to Claude's treasure first. The memory of Dr. Goodwin's voice and his menacing words gave me shivers even now. And the worst part was his palpable absence had me worried even more as to what he was up to.

***

Later that afternoon, I found Greta and Lily in the kitchen, Greta on her step-stool washing up and Lily reading the newspaper while sipping tea. Both still refused to use the new coffee machine. I sifted through a few of the drawers, looking for my favorite pen. "Done with the rooms already, Greta?"

Greta continued washing. "I tried, but Zippy was still sleeping off her hangover."

"Ziggy," I corrected.

"Whatever."

"The Smarty Pants rep will be over later to take a look at the settings for the door alarm. I want you both to stay out of his way, and you," I pointed at Greta, "don't give him any trouble. I don't want a repeat of what happened with the landscaper last month."

Greta grunted. "Suit yourself."

"Listen," I said, opening the third drawer in search of my pen. "I've got a fun surprise for both of you."

Lily eyed me sideways. "What kind of surprise? Your definition of fun often differs from mine."

I smiled broadly, trying to infuse as much positive energy into what I had to share. "We get to help Angie with the upcoming wedding."

Lily took a sip of her tea, then asked, "What's your definition of help?"

"Look, Angie needs us. A bunch of her caterers backed out, and she's in a tight spot. You both like Angie, right? Sweet, round lady? Always smells like cinnamon-sugar?"

"I'm unavailable." Lily returned to sipping her tea.

"And I'm shackled to this tracking device." Greta waved her ankle from atop her stool. "Can't chance going too far from the house or it might detonate."

"Don't be so dramatic," I said. "You're allowed to move around town." I rounded on Lily. "And you're infinitely available, so don't act so haughty. You've been languishing around this house for far too long. There's no use protesting because I already signed us up."

"I couldn't possibly serve people," Lily stammered out. "I've got my collection coming up, and—"

I closed the fourth drawer with extra force. "Don't start with *the collection*. You can manage a bit of hospitality on Angie's behalf. It's a paid gig and last I checked you don't have anything better going on."

Lily recoiled.

"And if you're having trouble bringing yourself to help out another human being, consider it repayment for your extended stay at my bed-and-breakfast."

That silenced her completely.

"Angie and Harper will be over tonight to go over the game plan, so be prepared."

"Fine," Lily said.

Greta huffed. "Suit yourself."

I nodded, satisfied that my message had gotten through. "Now, have either of you seen my favorite pen?"

***

Ziggy sat at a bench on the kitchen porch, looking worse for wear. Mayor Dewey brushed against and through her legs making a figure eight as he went. Daisy, Ryan's hideous mutt, lay in the grass on my lawn. The dog's tongue lolled through two snaggleteeth and the tuft of hair atop her head was particularly frizzy today.

"I see you've met our mayor," I said, catching her attention.

Ziggy looked up. Dark circles sagged under her eyes. "The mayor?" She ran a hand along Dewey's ginger fur. "How charming."

"And his partner in crime, Daisy." I motioned to the dog, who perked up at the mention of her name. "They basically have the run of the town."

"Well, if this guy's the mayor, he makes the rules, right?"

I chuckled. "I suppose so. How are you feeling today?"

Ziggy pulled her knees up and tucked them under her chin. "Better. Fuzzy. I keep thinking Charmaine is still here."

I placed a hand on her shoulder. "I'm very sorry for your loss."

"Thanks, I guess."

I sat down next to her. "You must have felt pretty awful last night. Clover mentioned that you left the room and spent some time in the bathroom."

Ziggy let out a forced laugh. "If she says so. I don't really remember much. I'm not much of a drinker so I guess it all went to my head."

Not much of a drinker? Ha! I kept my face still. "Do you remember anything from last night?"

"I think I remember passing out on the bathroom floor a few times. The floor was cold."

I repeated her words. "A few times?"

"Yeah, you know, in and out. I remember the cold floor felt good against my cheek. I must have been running hot."

I wondered how Ziggy could have managed much of anything in the state she was in last night. I'd seen her myself—stumbling, laughing, glassy-eyed. "Anything else you can remember?"

"I told your police guy everything, but it's all so fuzzy I can't be one hundred percent sure of it. I think eventually I stumbled back to my room. Gosh, that sounds terrible." She lay her forehead on her curled-up knees.

"We all drink a bit too much sometimes," I said. "You girls had a lot to catch up on. I'm sure it just got away from you."

She gave me a half-hearted smile. "You're sweet to say it."

"The pictures you all shared last night were a lot of fun. You sure look different."

"We're all going to look different than we did as kids. No one stays the same."

"Well, then, you certainly blossomed. You look so glamorous now." I caught myself on that last bit since Ziggy was not looking so glamorous at this moment—hair rolled into a messy bun and still in her pajamas, which I suspected were on backward.

"You really think so?"

"Sure, although you were beautiful in those pictures, too."

"All I see in those photos is frizzy hair and scrawny legs. An enormous nose. Next to Charmaine, I was a real ugly duckling."

"Charmaine didn't seem to have changed much."

The noise Ziggy made was a mix between a laugh and a scoff. "No, Charmaine definitely didn't change. Still the same Charmaine she'd always been—beautiful, cold, arrogant." Ziggy quickly looked at me, a worried expression on her face. "I'm sorry. That was rude."

I held up a hand. "It's okay. I got a taste of Charmaine, too."

Ziggy seemed relieved. "It's not that I wanted any harm to come to her, but she was a real bully and always has been. Had been, that is." She tucked her knees tighter.

"I'm sorry you went through that. I've faced bullies too. Were the others bullied as well?"

"Oh, sure. I think Maya and Clover have grown pretty resentful, but I suppose they all have. Except maybe Saffron." Ziggy shook her head. "I still can't figure out why she'd choose Charmaine as her Maid of Honor. Kismet has always been her best friend. Don't you think that's strange?"

Having just learned the details behind that particular kerfuffle, I chose to keep my response short. "Mm-hmm. Strange."

"I never would have guessed Charmaine as the Maid of Honor. If I had to guess, I'd say she would have been the *last* choice."

Last choice? That's not how Saffron made it sound.

Ziggy unfurled her legs and stood up. "I guess I should go put myself together and spend some time with the others. I appreciate your kind words."

"I'm glad you're feeling better. Let me know if you remember anything else."

As Ziggy returned inside, I remained on the side

porch. My mind raced around the contradiction of what Ziggy had revealed. Had Saffron been telling me the truth earlier? And if Charmaine wasn't an obvious second choice to Kismet, rather a *last* resort, why had she been selected?

"Alert. Alert. Front door alert."

My eyes rolled into an exasperated shudder before I realized who was probably at the door. "Finally."

Six

I MADE MY way along the wrap-around porch to the front landing just as the Smarty Pants technician stubbed out a cigarette under the toe of his boot.

One look at my flat stare and he picked it up then shoved the butt into a shirt pocket branded with the Smarty Pants logo. He tipped his cap. "Good afternoon. Heard you're having trouble with your alarm system?"

"That's right," I said. "I need the sensitivity turned down. And the smart toaster is acting up, too."

"Now, have you completed your settings in the online application?" His voice held more than a touch of condescension.

"I've completed all the settings, all the things. The door alarm sounded a bunch of times last night. I think Mayor Dewey kept setting it off."

He raised a bushy eyebrow. "The mayor?"

"Sorry. I meant the neighborhood cat."

"Gotcha. Why don't we take a look at the panel I installed? Any other issues with the system?"

"Not *yet*," I said with a grumble. "Follow me."

The Smarty Pants electrical hub he'd previously installed was in the kitchen, tucked behind the door that led to the basement.

"Alrighty then." He pulled a screwdriver from the toolbox he'd brought and popped open the box. He shone a small flashlight inside. "Nothing seems out of place here. Can I take a look at your app settings?"

I handed him my phone, and he pressed a few buttons. He hummed an indecipherable tune as he scrolled through the app. "Settings seem to be just fine. What did you want changed?"

"The sensitivity of the door alarm. I can't have it going off every time a bug flies by."

"Hmm." He scrunched his lips. "The sensitivity is set pretty low. It shouldn't be picking up anything that small."

"How about a cat?" I asked. "Or a small dog?"

"Eh, maybe, but I doubt it. This setting should only go off if a person, or maybe a kid, was at the door."

"Are you sure?"

"I can check the sensor outside, if you'd like?"

"Yes, please. Mayor Dewey has a tendency to prowl my porch in the wee hours."

"Why don't I take a look at that toaster first."

I led him to the nearby toaster then sort of flailed my hand at it in exasperation. "It won't toast correctly. Either raw bread or burnt to a crisp."

"Have you run the most recent update on the app?"

"The what?"

"The most recent update," he repeated. "There was a toaster software update recently and you'll need the most current update in order for this thing to function optimally."

"It's not even functioning barely."

"Try the update," he said with a confident nod. "I'll check out that sensor while you do that."

I followed him back out to the front porch, and he fiddled with the mounted sensor while I pulled up the app. *Not enough memory.* "Hey," I called to him. "It says I don't have enough memory for the update."

"Can't help you there. That's your phone's issue. Maybe you could delete a few things to make room?"

I grumbled in response and scrolled through my apps looking for unused programs to delete. I found an old puzzle game I didn't play anymore and chose to uninstall that.

A moment later, I pulled up the Smarty Pants app again and tried to install the update. *Not enough memory.* "Well, how much do I need?" I guessed I could delete that exercise app I never used, but I had all my stats programmed in already, and if I ever decided to take up speed walking again, I'd have to enter them all over. Better to delete the weather app that always thought I lived in Romania.

"Okay." The technician tightened the last screw on the sensor mount and stepped back. "I didn't find anything off with the sensor, so I'm not sure what's been tripping it. I guess if a gull flew up and fluttered around in front of it." He waved his arms wildly, impersonating one of these supposed flailing sea pigeons.

"I have never seen a gull on this porch."

"Welp," he said, shaking his head. "Can't explain it. Maybe my little fiddle here shook it out of its funk. Give it a night, and if you still have problems, I'll come back out and replace the whole thing."

As frustrated as I was, if the technician couldn't find anything wrong, then I'd have to let it be and hope for the best. I turned the settings on and decided to give it a try. I could always turn it back off if things got crazy. Another night of incessant alarms would be the death of me. And we'd already had enough death in this house.

***

"Alert. Alert. Front door alert."

I swung the front door open to find Angie, arms laden with mounds of black fabric. Harper, holding Mayor Dewey in her arms, slumped inside after her, feet shuffling as if held down by weights of obligation.

I quickly ushered them into the library off the foyer and Angie dumped the load of black clothing into one of the two matching club chairs.

Greta and Lily soon joined us and I shut the door behind them, leaving my guests to themselves.

"What's all this?" I asked.

"Uniforms," Angie said. "We'll all wear these during the rehearsal dinner and for the reception."

Lily immediately turned to leave, but I held out an arm to block her way. She could not have mistaken my one raised eyebrow for anything other than a clear directive. She turned around and eased herself into the remaining club chair, crossed her legs elegantly, and stared forward.

Angie patted her stomach and let out a big breath. "I practically tripped over Mayor Dewey on my way in. I guess I couldn't see him over the pile of clothes."

Harper rocked Mayor Dewey like a baby. His eyes were half-lidded, and he barely moved a furry muscle. "He was waiting right by the door as we walked up."

"Really?" I asked in surprise. "The alarm didn't go off."

"Should it have?" Angie seemed surprised at my surprise.

"No," I said. "I suppose not." A small relief washed over me. Maybe the alarm was working correctly after all? I looked forward to a good night sleep, but then I spotted Greta thumbing through an old book and I remembered that my living arrangements weren't ideal. Hopefully, this catering gig would give Lily just the right amount of discomfort to push her out of my house forever.

"All right," Angie said. "Let's get started. It's late already."

Harper checked her watch. "It's five-thirty."

"Well, that's late for a baker. Anyway, these are the uniforms you'll be wearing, so find your size and grab a shirt and a pair of the pants."

Harper pawed at the pile. "What a joke—there aren't even pockets. And none of these will fit Mayor Dewey."

Angie set her fists on her hips. "Mayor Dewey will go nowhere near the catering, got it? That goes for Daisy as well."

"You'll have to tell Ryan that," Harper said. "I'm only Dewey's assistant."

"Isn't Ethan MacKenzie supposed to be Daisy's keeper?" Angie asked.

Harper shrugged. "I don't know. Daisy seems pretty keeperless these days. Hey, Poppy, you should talk to those MacKenzie boys about that."

"I did. They try to keep a handle on her, but I'll mention it again." Poor Daisy. Ryan's recent adoption of her had been rooted in kindness, but she was a little rascal, and Ethan had school during the day, so he couldn't watch her. Honestly, I think Mayor Dewey was a bad influence, and probably was the dominant force in their terrorization of the town. He seemed innocent now, cradled like a log in Harper's arms, but he'd been known to get up to trouble.

"All right, everyone, listen up." While Angie's voice held a smidge of force, coming from such a tiny dumpling of a person, it was comical. "Food service requires a high degree of responsibility, customer focus, and tact."

All eyes swiveled to Greta.

She picked something from her teeth. "What?"

Angie sighed and continued. "We'll be starting with the rehearsal dinner at the community center. In addition to the dinner Shelby and I will prepare, you four will be making the rounds serving hors d'oeuvres."

Greta cleared her throat. "And exactly what percentage of these nibbles will we be able to eat?"

Angie rounded on Greta. "You will eat exactly zero."

"What if I'm asked for a recommendation? If I haven't tried it, how can I recommend it?"

"You won't need to recommend them," Angie said. "They are appetizers. They will get eaten."

Greta shrugged. "Suit yourself, but if anyone asks me, I'll have to tell them I was warned not to try them."

Angie pinched the bridge of her nose. "Maybe it's best if Greta sits this one out."

"Absolutely not," I said in a low growl directed

Greta's way.

After a few minutes, Angie had run through the rules and expectations of our catering tasks. It seemed pretty straightforward to me, but I worried that neither Greta, Lily, nor Harper had listened to a word of it. Carry trays, when the trays are empty, get another tray, rinse and repeat. "Don't worry, Angie. We'll get you through this." I turned to the lukewarm faces of the other three women and spoke through gritted teeth. "We're happy to help."

Lily rose from her cemented spot in the club chair in one lithe movement. "Since we're done here, you'll excuse me before I die of boredom."

After the door shut behind my sister. Greta was the first to speak. "What I want to know is, when do we get access to the church? That X on the wall marked the spot and we need to investigate."

I took Lily's vacated spot in the club chair. "Pastor Basil will be preoccupied with the rehearsal tomorrow."

Angie squirmed. "I hate the idea of snooping around."

"We won't be *snooping*," Harper said. "We're just going to take a good hard look around the church, right Poppy?"

"Hmm, right. I'd like to know what Greta thinks Everett Goodwin and the Gold Hand's next move will be. We'll need to be careful."

"With the wall exposed, it won't be long until they realize what it means, whether they have Claude Goodwin's map or not. They'll make a move sooner or later and we should be prepared."

"Should we stake out the church?" Harper asked.

I practically snorted. "Lovie would get a kick out of

that."

"Well, I'm certainly not staking anything out," Angie said. "I can barely keep my eyes open past eight o'clock."

Greta picked at her teeth again. "I can do it."

My response was immediate. "Not a chance. Snooping around the church late at night is exactly what you shouldn't be doing in *that*." I pointed to her ankle monitor. "Deputy Todd would have a field day."

"Okay," Harper said. "No staking out the church, but I don't like the idea of the Gold Hand skulking around. They give me the creeps."

"We'll just have to keep our eyes and ears open," I said. "The last thing we want is to get caught off guard."

Seven

THE FOLLOWING MORNING, Greta and I hiked up the stairs to service the suites after breakfast. We started with the large Victorian suite in which Saffron now occupied alone.

I stripped the sheets off the large, intricately carved bed. "Maya's yoga class is later this morning. You could join us, you know."

"Hoo-ee," Greta said. "That's just asking for a gaseous explosion. Best not."

"You're right," I said, suddenly thankful I'd escaped a dire fate. I was still recovering from the previous night's gaseous explosions. "Never mind."

Greta fluffed the pillows while I plugged in the vacuum. I set the dustbin aside and pushed and pulled the vacuum across the rug underneath the bed.

"Zippy was at breakfast," Greta said. "That means we'll finally be able to clean that room."

"Ziggy."

"Whatever. She didn't eat anything. Little twig of a

woman, isn't she?"

"Don't talk about the guests."

"Pfft. That's rich coming from you."

"I'm not about to take any guff from you," I said. "Don't think I didn't notice one of my ceramic birds was missing from the kitchen window sill this morning. You should have told me you broke it."

"I didn't break your little birdie."

My lips twisted in frustration at her lie, but I continued vacuuming. A moment later the vacuum caught, whirring with a terrible sound of clanking and grinding. I quickly shut off the machine.

Greta rushed over. "What was that? Sounded like you ran a rock through a shredder."

I tipped the vacuum upside down and checked the intake. Trapped between the machine's fringes and strands of hair wound around the rotator were two halves of what once was a delicate rosy pink stone. Once buffed to a high shine, they now had a number of scuffs and mars from the rock's run through the vacuum, not to mention the ragged edge where it had cleaved in two.

I held one piece up to the window. Even with the scratches the sunlight made it glow.

"Do you know anything about rocks or crystals?" I asked Greta.

"Course I don't. Bunch of hogwash. We should bury those. She doesn't have to know it was us."

I frowned. "Did you bury my ceramic bird after you broke it, too?"

"I didn't break your stupid bird, but suit yourself. You're welcome to tell that lady you ruined her shiny rock."

I hated to admit to a guest that I'd broken something of theirs, but it's not like I could pretend it didn't happen. "I'll have to tell Saffron I'm sure she'll understand. It was laying under the bed, after all."

"Bit odd, don't you think? Dropping that sparkly stone and not picking it up. Who would do that?"

Greta made a good point. "Kismet mentioned that Saffron may have used crystals in a secret ritual. I wonder if these had anything to do with that? I'll ask her about it later. For now, we need to straighten up the rest of these rooms before I head off to yoga, or else you'll be doing it all yourself."

As Greta kicked into high gear, I slipped the rosy stones into my pocket. With a murder happening in this very room just a couple of days ago, anything strange was worth looking into.

***

Angie hurried across the street from the bakery to the community center, where I waited outside for others to arrive. She'd changed from her usual baker's garb and apron into a very tight pair of eye-popping spandex pants and a floury T-shirt. Her cheeks fumed red, and she smacked a rolled-up newspaper into my hand. "That Valentine woman really boils my bagels."

"Oh no." I unfurled the newspaper and read the article.

Body Count Rises at Starry Cove's Murder Mansion

Another day, another death at Starry Cove's most

dangerous dwelling. The Pearl-by-the-Sea bed-and-breakfast was the site of yet another gruesome murder, ending the promising life of a young entrepreneur.

Authorities were called to the murder mansion in the early hours of the morning, where the victim's body lay cold in an upstairs bedroom.

In addition to the seven other guests, also present was Greta (last name unavailable), a live-in employee who flashed her ankle monitor proudly. It remains unclear what connection there may be between the mononymous criminal and the sudden, unexplained murder.

Poppy Lewis, tight-lipped proprietress of the infamous bed-and-breakfast, had no comment other than to indicate that law enforcement incompetence, particularly on the part of Sheriff Deputy Todd Newman, may be to blame for the recent spate of horrifying homicides.

I groaned. "Great. No chance Deputy Todd hasn't seen this already."

"She's just awful. And what she insinuated about Greta." Angie huffed. "I'm just so mad."

"Mad about what?" Maya appeared next to us. A rolled-up yoga mat was slung in a case over her shoulder.

I hid the newspaper behind my back. "Nothing. Just general anger, you know?"

Maya cocked her head and didn't appear convinced. "I've got good news for you then. Yoga is great for general anger." She winked and headed through the open double doors into the community center.

We followed her in and soon enough everyone had arrived, including all of my other guests—minus Jennifer—and a few of the townspeople who'd heard about the morning session.

Harper rushed in last, dressed head-to-toe in rainbow workout gear, complete with rainbow leg warmers. She peered over the heads filling the room. "Is Charlie here yet?"

Angie and I smiled. "She's up there," I said, pointing to the front.

"Sweet. I'll catch you both later." She rushed off and found a spot next to the stunning brunette.

Maya clapped, catching everyone's attention. "Thank you all for joining me. Please take a seat on your mats and we'll begin."

We started with gentle neck stretching, around and around, side to side. In the silence between Maya's instructions, my mind wandered to the unexplained issues surrounding Charmaine's death.

"If your mind wanders," Maya intoned, "simply bring it back to your breathing."

Oops.

"Let's move into the Downward-facing Dog position."

I contorted myself into an inverted V shape, which made me think of Veronica Valentine and her article. I was sure Deputy Todd was already planning his attack on me. *Murder mansion? That won't be good for marketing. Everything's going sideways. And the new Smarty Pants features weren't going to be the boon I hoped they'd be, either. Greta was such a Luddite. I really need to get that app updated. And do laundry.*

"If your mind wanders, bring it back to your breath."
Dang it.

"Warrior One pose." Maya demonstrated, stretching her arms high, lean muscles in perfect form. "Hold for thirty seconds."

Out of the corner of my eye, I spotted one of the bridesmaids sliding effortlessly into the pose. She shook her head once, tossing her long blonde braid over her shoulder.

Heavenleigh? No, long hair. That's Saffron. Hmm. Saffron's secret ritual. A crystal under her bed. Maid of Honor shenanigans. My eyes narrowed as Saffron's inhaled a deep breath, totally relaxed.

I felt the ache building in my arms as Maya moved us into Warrior Two.

A moment into the pose a slight commotion broke my concentration on my breathing. Ziggy had toppled over while shifting poses. Clover and Kismet were already helping her up, and she laughed it off with an awkward giggle.

I returned to Warrior Two. *Is Ziggy still drunk? There's no way someone that hammered could have taken out Charmaine. Charmaine would have eaten her for breakfast. Clover and Kismet, though. Those two didn't bother to hide their hatred and were a lot less flimsy than Ziggy.*

"If you find your mind wandering, recenter on your breathing."

Shoot. There was simply too much running through my head.

Maya walked the room, observing. She stopped next to Angie and adjusted Angie's stout form, straightening her arms.

My friend was about to pop—red, sweaty, struggling to keep it together. She burst out a heavy breath when Maya released us from the pose. A wave of relief passed over her face when Maya instructed us to sit down for our cool-down.

"As you move into Lotus Pose," Maya said in a soft, soothing voice, "I want you to thank yourself for taking the time to be here today. For taking the time for yourself, loving yourself."

Thank you, Poppy, for loving yourself.

Despite my wandering thoughts, I finished the session with a relaxed body, if not a relaxed mind.

Harper and Angie had already left by the time Maya approached me as I rolled up my yoga mat. "Feeling less general anger, I hope?"

"Oh, yes," I replied. "Feeling much better. It's amazing what a little stretching and posing can do for your mindset."

Maya nodded knowingly.

"It's amazing you have time for this. I'd think you'd be incredibly busy as a doctor."

"There's always time to care for yourself. Besides, I find that yoga is the perfect activity to exercise my body and focus on mindfulness. It keeps me grounded." She glanced toward the open double doors of the community center, where the other bridesmaids had exited. "I just hope it helps the others heal."

"Did it help you heal?" I asked her.

She sighed. "Yes, as much as it could. There are

wounds no amount of yoga could heal."

"What do you mean?"

Maya hefted her yoga mat more firmly onto her shoulder. "My relationship with Charmaine was rough. It was rough for all of us."

"Is there any particular reason?"

"This sounds bad, but I think Charmaine may have been a little jealous of my success. I don't want that to come across as conceited."

"Not at all. Charmaine seemed the type to want to be number one all the time."

Maya laughed. "You nailed it. Growing up, we were like any group of girls. We laughed, we fought. We held grudges. I can't say I was happy to see her after all these years, but I think it's awful what happened. She had a lot of enemies, though."

"Anyone specific?"

Maya chuckled again. "Everyone."

I nodded, not surprised at Maya's take on Charmaine's relationships. "What about that night? Is there anything you remember that stood out?"

Maya considered my question for a moment, then said, "I don't think it means anything, but Heavenleigh left our room to use the restroom, something about a sensitive stomach. She told me she might be awhile."

This surprised me, since I'd heard from others that Ziggy had hogged the restroom most of the night. "Are you sure?"

"Yeah, why?"

I waved it off. "Never mind. It's nothing. I'll close up here if you need to go."

"Thanks. There are a few things I want to take care

of before the rehearsal this afternoon."

After Maya left, I closed up the community center, still churning Heavenleigh and Ziggy's bathroom paradox in my mind. Something wasn't fitting.

Mind occupied, I stepped from the community center walkway onto the sidewalk and ran right into a strange man. "Oh, I'm so sorry."

"No, no," he said. "I'm the one who startled you."

He stood tall with broad shoulders and a full head of sandy curls that blew in the salty wind off the ocean.

Something seemed familiar, but I couldn't quite place him. "Do I know you from somewhere?"

"I don't think so," he said with a charming smile. "But you do now." He held out his hand. "Benjamin Locke. I just took over the bookstore down the street."

"Of course!" I shook his hand in greeting. "I'm Poppy Lewis. I run the bed-and-breakfast at the roundabout into town." I gestured down the street toward the Pearl.

"The murder mansion?"

My face and shoulders dropped, but he only laughed.

"I'm kidding," he said. "That reporter writes like a tabloid. Next thing you know, we'll have alien abductions along Main Street. I am sorry to hear about your troubles, though."

"Thanks. So, how are you liking Starry Cove so far? I came by the bookstore earlier and peeked in, but it's all closed up."

"It's a bit of a mess still. Not quite ready. As for Starry Cove..." He peered up and down the street before returning to look at me and smiled. "It's suddenly looking quite lovely."

I hoped the flush from yoga hid my blush. "Um, I'm sure you'll find that it's a wonderful town."

"No doubt. Well, I should get back to the store. It was great to meet you, Poppy Lewis."

I waved weakly, twiddling my fingers as Benjamin strode down the sidewalk and out of sight. I realized I'd been holding my breath and let it out with a whoosh. My cheeks felt hot, and I leaned against the sidewalk fence. *Uh oh.*

***

I spoke with no one about my flirtation with Benjamin Locke. Instead, I occupied myself with deep cleaning the common room. I picked up all the Klover Kombucha bottles, straightened the wonky sofa cushions, and set out a new pine-scented candle to replace one that had been misplaced or discarded.

I'd just lit the new candle when the door alarm went off on my phone. Saffron, Clover, Kismet, and Heavenleigh filed in through the door laughing with a few gift bags dangling off their arms.

"Where did you four go?" I asked with genuine curiosity.

Heavenleigh dropped her bags into a nearby chair. "We wanted to check out a few shops and get some last-minute things for the wedding. We just left a charming little shop off the highway."

"Was it the Treasures of the Coast? My friend owns that shop."

"Does she?" Heavenleigh asked. "It was delightful. So many precious things to look at."

"I could have spent a fortune there," Clover said.

"Thankfully, I kept my wallet locked up tight. I should have taken some kombucha, though."

"You and your kombucha," Kismet said with a snicker. "I'm going upstairs to get ready for the rehearsal."

"Me too," Clover said, following Kismet up the stairs.

Heavenleigh picked up her bags and sat down in the same chair, spreading her flowy sundress out over her legs. She dug into one of the bags and pulled out a small carved redwood figurine. "It's a gnome. I got it at your friend's shop. Isn't it adorable? I love gnomes."

"It's really cute."

She smiled down at the carving, then placed it back into her bag.

"Not getting ready with the others?" I asked her.

"Me? No, I'm not really a 'get ready' kind of person."

"Are you excited to be a bridesmaid?"

"Sure. I mean, Saffron and I were friends, but we aren't very close now. I was a bit surprised when she asked me, but I'm happy to be a part of it. I just hope she didn't feel obligated."

"Obligated? Why's that?"

Heavenleigh dropped her hands to her lap. "You may not have heard, but my father is the founder of Bliss Ridge where we all grew up. I wondered if she asked me because I'm *that* girl. Like, obligated, so she didn't offend him. I've always had to wonder that growing up. Who's really my friend or just pretending."

"I'm sure Saffron's not pretending. She seemed genuinely happy to have you here."

Heavenleigh flashed a beautiful smile. "I hope you're right, but I suspect it's the reason Clover asked if my father and I were interested in investing in her company. I don't think she wanted Papa Zamora to miss out on the opportunity."

"I thought Charmaine was her investor?" It hit me right after I'd said it. "But I guess that's an issue now."

"Well, it seemed like a strange request because neither of us have any investing experience."

"I'm sure it was just Clover wanting to share the opportunity."

"Again, I hope you're right. I've always loved these girls." She sniffed the air. "What is that smell?"

"I just lit a pine candle. Is it bothering you?"

"No, it's lovely," Heavenleigh said. "Why would it bother me?"

"Maya mentioned that you had some sensitivities."

Heavenleigh nodded as if this question came up frequently. "Gluten. It messes with my tummy, but smells don't bother me."

"I'm sorry to hear that. Maya said you were in the restroom for a while that first night."

She cringed. "I needed some private time."

Gluten allergy. Private time. So, which one of them was in the bathroom, Ziggy or Heavenleigh? One of them had to be lying. "I'll be sure to let Greta know about your dietary needs for breakfast."

"Please don't make a fuss over me," Heavenleigh said. "I've learned to live around it."

"You should ask Maya for a referral."

"Maya? I never considered her. You don't think… You don't think she could have done something while I was in the restroom, do you?"

If *you were using the restroom, that is.* "Did anything seem odd when you returned to your room?"

She considered for a quick moment. "No, and I'm pretty sure she'd fallen asleep. I tried to be quiet when I returned."

Tried to be stealthy, you mean. "I wouldn't worry about it then. Did you enjoy her yoga this morning? I found it very relaxing."

Heavenleigh threw back her head and shook out her short blonde hair. "I absolutely *loved* it. She's a really great yogi, isn't she? Her talents are wasted as a doctor."

We both laughed at the absurdity of it.

"What's so funny?"

We both turned as Saffron entered the common room.

"We're laughing at Maya's expense," Heavenleigh said. "She's too good a yogi to be a doctor."

"Poor Maya," Saffron said with jest. "Always picked on. Are you about ready to go, Heavenleigh? The others should be down in a minute."

Heavenleigh popped up from the chair and grabbed her bags. "I'll leave these upstairs and be right down."

"We're leaving you with an empty house, Poppy," Saffron said.

My stomach tied into a knot. Harper, Angie, and I would be conducting our covert operation around the church during the rehearsal. "I'll be helping my friend with serving at the rehearsal dinner, so I'll see you there."

"All right, we'll catch you then." Saffron took Heavenleigh's arm and the two blondes sauntered away, swaying in time and laughing in unison.

A twinge rose in my stomach. I just hoped they didn't catch me snooping.

***

I met Harper and Angie in front of the bookstore. The wedding rehearsal was well underway, so all participants were safely stowed inside the Fellowship of the Faith church across the street.

From my vantage point, I could clearly make out the cobblestone wall and the mark literally marking the spot of what we all hoped was Claude Goodwin's treasure.

Harper rubbed her hands together. "Let's get going. I'm ready to finally get my hands on this gold."

"I've only got an hour before I need to get back to the bakery. If I keep the away sign up for too long, Mrs. Perez will sound the alarm. She doesn't like to wait for her sticky buns. Plus, I still have so much prep work for the rehearsal dinner tonight."

I spared a peek into the bookstore, but it was dark and nothing moved within sight of my peep hole.

"Have you met the new owner yet?" Angie asked.

I tried to suppress a smile. "I ran into him earlier."

Harper squinted at me. "Why are you smiling?"

"What's he like?" Angie asked. "Lovie and Shelby both said he's really handsome, and he's a really hard worker trying to get that bookstore back open."

My half-hearted shrug hid nothing. "He's nice."

"You're holding back," Harper said. "Fess up."

I crossed my arms. "I'm not sure what you mean."

"You've got crush written all over your face."

"I do not."

Angie took a short step forward and squinted up at

me. "You're blushing."

"Am not."

Harper closed in, pinning me against the bookstore wall. "Tell us *everything*."

I gulped. "There's not much to tell. I ran into him after yoga. He introduced himself—Benjamin Locke—and said he was really liking Starry Cove so far."

Harper's eye twitched.

"And that he thought I was lovely." I couldn't help but grin letting that last part out.

Angie gaped. "He didn't? How bold."

Harper nodded appreciatively. "I knew you were holding back."

"Forget about it. He was just being nice, and anyway, my heart belongs to Ryan. He seemed oddly familiar though, like I'd met him before."

"I hope he stops by the bakery. I wonder if he likes cinnamon rolls."

"Everyone likes cinnamon rolls," Harper said. "C'mon. This treasure isn't going to find itself."

We crossed Main Street and approached the church.

"Let's get a close look at the mark first," I said.

Harper led us through the church garden to the stone wall recently cleared of ivy. "There may be a loose rock or something."

"Don't crush Pastor Basil's bulbs," I said, "or you'll be sorry."

"I can only reach the first four feet," Angie said, hopping to touch the highest stones she could.

Harper and I ran our hands around the various stones, looking for some imperfection, crack, or secret panel. Harper, the tallest, was able to reach seven feet off the ground, but even with her height, we couldn't inspect the higher stones.

"There's at least another two-thirds we can't get to," Harper said. "Do they look the same to you?"

I held my hand up to my eyes like a visor. "Yeah. They don't seem any different. I think we're on the wrong track."

"Does that mean I can stop searching?" Angie pulled up from her hands and knees, mud scuffing her apron where her knees had been. "I didn't find anything, either."

"I don't like this," I said. "There's no way Claude would have made it so simple."

"Simple?" Harper guffawed. "We've been searching for this treasure forever."

"You know what I mean. He wouldn't hide a few coins behind a false wall. That's too easy. Too obvious. Greta surmised that he's probably entombed himself here, and that's not going to be in a wall."

Harper rubbed the dirt and dust from her hands. "If you say so."

"It must be inside somewhere."

"Well, we can't go inside," Angie said. "Pastor Basil will be onto us in a second."

I plopped down on a nearby garden bench. "We may need to wait until the wedding to get a better look. I hate to think of letting those Gold Hand goons have more time, but what can we do?"

"Nothing would give me more satisfaction right now than to rip up the floor in this church and dive into a pool of gold."

"Harper…" Angie said. "Have some respect."

I railed off what we knew so far. "We know Claude

Goodwin stole his grandfather's pirate gold. He left us a map and marked this spot with an X. We suspect he's entombed himself somewhere nearby."

"Probably directly under the pulpit," Harper said with a groan.

"I'm not pulling up the pulpit," Angie said. "This is our *church*."

"*Your* church," Harper corrected.

"Enough," I said. "We'll have a chance to poke around after the wedding. That may be our best bet. Everyone will have cleared out and Pastor Basil will be away at the reception."

"I'm in," Harper said. "Angie?"

"I hate to remind you both, but you're catering with me during the wedding reception."

Ugh. I had forgotten.

"What about tonight?" Harper asked. "Pastor Basil doesn't even have to know if we take a peek inside."

"I thought we agreed we wouldn't?"

"It might be our only option now," I said. "How about after the rehearsal dinner?"

Harper nodded.

Angie frowned and bit her lip. "I'll be dead tired."

"Does that mean you're in?" Harper asked.

She let out a huffy sigh. "I guess I'm in."

Eight

THE EVENING OF the rehearsal dinner rolled around and all my guests rushed about like chickens.

I'd already dressed into my uniform when I swung through the swivel door into the kitchen. Lily sat at the table scrolling furtively on her phone, brow furrowed into deep creases. She also wore her catering uniform, but somehow managed to appear more elegant than I did, form-fitted in just the right places.

"It won't be that bad," I said. "You don't have to look so sour."

"What?" Lily looked up as if surprised to find me there. She waved me off and returned to her phone. "It's not that."

"What are you doing then?" I asked.

She didn't look up. "Research."

"For what?"

"My collection."

"What's to research?"

Lily dropped the phone to her lap and gave me a dead

stare. "Why all the questions?"

"Just curious. Won't it be great to get back to your own place and finally be out of here?"

"Yes."

"You're not much for conversation," I said.

"I'm being peppered with questions. It's not a conversation."

"Yeesh, sorry." I turned away with a roll of my eyes, grabbed the kettle and filled it with water. The lid clanked as I set it on the burner.

"Would you please keep it down?" Lily demanded.

"Something bothering you?" I asked. "You're awfully testy."

"It's none of your—. Never mind."

"It's none of my what? Business? You've been living in my house—"

"Uncle Arthur's house."

"The house he left to *me*. You have been living here free as a bird waiting on this collection to drop, whenever that's happening, so please tell me what isn't my business."

Lily pressed the back of her hand to her forehead. "Stop, please. I'm feeling ill."

I balked. "Don't play that game with me."

Her hand dropped, and she stared daggers. "Fine."

"So," I said, "what's really going on? You looked worried when I walked in."

I could tell she was mulling words over in her head. She kept moving to speak, but then stopped. I didn't prompt her. I didn't goad her. I just waited.

Finally, she spoke. "I suppose it's time I tell you. The collection is my—"

The kitchen door to the porch flew open and Angie and Harper spilled through in their matching black uniforms.

"Everybody ready?" Angie asked, looking from me to Lily. "Where's Greta?"

"She's changing," I said. "I don't think I've ever seen her wearing pants."

"I hope they're on straight," Harper mumbled.

Angie waved an arm toward the porch. "Which of your guests is the smoker? They left a mess outside."

"What?" I asked in surprise.

"There's a pile of cigarette butts outside."

Harper flopped down in a nearby chair. "I can't believe you'd let guests smoke after that actor guy almost burned down the Pearl."

"I *don't* let them." Then I remembered catching the Smarty Pants technician smoking yesterday. "I think it was the smart home installer. He was here for a while installing everything. Probably smoked up a storm."

Lily scoffed, then mumbled under her breath, "Smart toaster…"

"You should get that mess cleaned up," Harper said.

Angie cut in. "It'll have to wait. Where's Greta? We need to get going."

As if on cue, Greta kicked through the swivel door from the dining room and entered the kitchen with a swagger. Thumbs hooked into the belt loops of her black catering pants, she waltzed in with a smug smile on her face. The trouser hems were rolled up into thick cuffs to account for her small stature, leaving the monitoring device bulging at her ankle. She snapped the cuffs at each wrist, which had been rolled up the same as her pants.

"Looks good, eh?"

"Looks like you have an ankle goiter," Harper said.

Greta admired her ankle monitor. "Better than your toothpick legs."

"What took you so long?" I asked.

"I was listening to that Kizzy lady smoochy-smooching on the phone."

"You were *what?*"

"It's the most action I've had in decades. '*Oh, Gardener, you say the naughtiest things.*' Anyway, we ready to hit the town? I've got a bunch of pent-up energy fighting to get out."

"Hold on," I said. "Who was Kismet talking to?"

Greta shrugged. "Some fella, I suppose. I only overheard one side of that telephone rendezvous, but it was steamier than a Norwegian sauna." She mimed fanning herself.

Harper turned away from Greta. "I might actually barf."

"Can we talk about this later?" Angie asked.

Harper shut her eyes tight. "How about never?"

Angie waved us toward the door. "We've got to get to the community center. Shelby's already there with all the food."

We filed through one by one. I made up the rear of our catering train, and along the walk, all I could think about was Kismet's telephone smoochy-smooch with a man definitely not named her husband.

***

Shelby yanked Angie to the back of the large community center room as soon as we arrived. We scurried after and stopped by a large table set up with plates, silverware, and warming trays. The rehearsal dinner had yet to start, and no guests had arrived, leaving our motley catering crew alone.

"Good gracious, dearies," Shelby said. "It's chaos. We've got to get things moving, lickety-split, otherwise the cream sauce will seize up and we can't have that, dearies. Mason!" Shelby waved over pimple-faced diner employee Mason, whose morose expression meant he must have been wrangled into catering like the rest of us. "I've been cooking all day, dearies, and we're barely sneaking in under the gun."

"She's been a real taskmaster," Mason said with a cracking voice.

Shelby shot him a look. "Look smart, Mason, and you might just walk away with a few tips tonight."

Greta was suddenly front and center. "Tips?"

Lily eyed Greta sideways and stepped forward, blocking the shorter woman. "What's this about tips?"

"There's a whole gaggle of folks who'll be here tonight, dearies. And each and every one of them understands the expectation that you tip the waitstaff. It's common courtesy."

Harper, too, seemed interested in what Shelby had to say. "I bet the drunker they are, the more they tip."

Greta, Harper, and Lily all glanced at a far table that supported the liquor and other alcoholic beverages. I could practically see the gears turning in their heads.

"Follow me, ladies," Mason croaked. "I'll show you where everything is."

Soon enough, we'd been prepped on trays and appetizers and drinks and all the other tidbits we needed to know for the night. Just as I was feeling prepared, the first guests arrived and took their seats.

Lily, Greta, and Harper rushed to grab wine bottles and descended upon the first guests with gusto, shoving reds and whites and bubbly champagne in their faces.

As the guests trickled in, I made my own rounds, serving food and collecting used plates and glasses. The bridal party arrived fashionably late, led by Kismet and her husband. Although they walked in arm-in-arm, there were no affectionate glances, definitely no smoochy-smooch. I felt a pang of sorrow for Kismet. I knew exactly how it felt to survive a spousal betrayal, but I also wondered who she'd been talking to earlier. Who was this Gardener fellow?

"More stuffed mushrooms, dearie?"

"Huh?" I turned to find Shelby tugging the empty tray from my hands and replacing it with one overflowing with gooey stuffed mushrooms.

An uproarious applause brought me back as Saffron and Chad finally made their entrance. Angie and Shelby said when they arrived the real dinner would start, so the catering team regrouped in the back of the room.

"All right, team," Angie said, waving her tongs like a baton, "we're at the main event."

Greta rubbed her hands together. "They're all lubed up pretty good. We could serve them rubber tires and they'd be satisfied."

Angie stomped a tiny foot. "No rubber tires. Shelby and I will serve the head table, the rest of you, start preparing your plates. And no funny business."

"Why are you looking at me?" Greta asked.

"Get going." Angie shooed us away.

The remainder of the guests took their seats and like the others, I made my way around the room serving dinner and offering the remainder of the appetizers. Harper, Greta, and Lily hogged the drink service, so I kept to the food.

While serving plates to a table near the head table, my ear caught a snippet of conversation between two guests.

"I heard the bride fainted during the rehearsal," the first woman said.

"No way," the second responded. "That doesn't bode well for the marriage, does it? It's a bad omen."

"And one of the bridesmaids was already *drunk*. Chad should run now. He's about to make a big mistake marrying into that dumpster fire commune family."

"Mm-hmm." The second woman smiled smugly. "Did you hear about Sylvia?"

The women's conversation quickly turned to Sylvia's botched nose job, and I moved on to the next table.

Drunk bridesmaid? I spotted Ziggy slumped at the end of the table reserved for the bridal party. Harper poured her a full glass of red wine.

Lily scooted in behind Harper, offering Ziggy her white wine. Ziggy reached across the table and grabbed Clover's empty water glass and shoved it under the white wine bottle.

Lily's smile broadened. "What lovely earrings you're wearing tonight. So classy."

"What?" Ziggy said with a slur. "These things?" She swiped at one dangly earring and it jangled into her hair. "I think Saffron gave them to me."

Lily topped off the second glass. "They are

absolutely *gorgeous*."

They were absolutely hideous.

Lily moved down the line of bridesmaids and offered wine to Kismet, and then Maya, all with a whirl and a flourish. Really laying it on thick. "You have to share where you got that *gorgeous* necklace?"

"This?" Maya grasped the delicate gold chain in her hands. "Thanks. I almost wore my late mother's necklace, but I thought this one looked best."

Lily rested her free hand over her heart. "Aw, how sweet. This one is just perfect, though."

I flinched. *How sweet?* Lily had never said those two words before in her life. Her competitive side was showing so much she was actually resorting to *kindness* to get the most tips.

Greta voice cackled from the groom's family's table. "You've got some great gams, lady. More wine?"

Mama Beige, Jennifer's mother, recoiled at the sight of Greta.

Ziggy had seen it too, and broke out laughing like a braying horse and flailed her arms exuberantly with every guffaw. I rushed to her side in time to catch her red wine before it spilled across Angie's crisp, white tablecloth.

"She's a funny one, that housekeeper of yours."

I could smell the alcohol seeping from her pores. Maya wasn't in her seat at the table, so I scanned the room for her, hoping she could help me get Ziggy back to the Pearl, but she was nowhere to be found, so I propped Ziggy up with my arm and waited. "Are you all right?"

"Me?" Hiccup. "Just dandy. Hey, that lady looks a lot like Jennifer, doesn't she?"

"That's Jennifer's mother."

"Is it?" Ziggy squinted, but I was sure she wasn't seeing anything clearly at this point. "I can't tell. Are there two of her or three?"

"One."

"Are you sure? Maybe Jennifer's next to her. That's two."

"Nope, still one."

"I really like Jennifer, don't you? She's so simple. She just fades into the background like a, um, faded background."

"She's a very nice woman."

Ziggy reached for the glass of red wine, but I shifted it out of her reach. "I knew I liked her the minute she gave Charmaine the stink eye."

"She gave Charmaine the stink eye?"

Hiccup. "Yep. I saw them talking that first night. Seemed pretty intense. Then there it was—the stink eye. I guess we all hated Charmaine, even someone who'd just met her." Ziggy burbled a half-laugh, half-cough, then whispered, "I hate you, Charmaine."

"What was that?" I asked.

"Huh?" Ziggy fumbled to sit up straight. "Oh, sorry. I shouldn't have said that out loud. I hate Charmaine. Oof." She wobbled in her chair. "Did it again. I guess I need an alibi." Hiccup. "Kombucha was there."

"Kombucha? Do you mean Clover?"

Ziggy slapped a hand clumsily on the table. "That's her."

"Don't worry," I said. "Clover told me she saw you head to the bathroom."

Ziggy looked at me sideways. "Huh? No, that can't be right." She shook her head and blew a raspberry.

"Clover wasn't there."

I was getting confused trying to piece together Ziggy's drunken thoughts. "You just said she was."

"Did I?" Ziggy stared off as if trying to remember. "Oh, I said she was there when I came back. Not when I left."

"Clover wasn't in the room when you left for the bathroom, only when you returned later?"

Ziggy frowned. "Say that one more time, slower."

I emphasized each word and asked again, "Was Clover in your room when you left?"

She nodded. "No"

"Is that a yes or a no?"

"No." Ziggy's face lit up. "There's my Maya-bear."

Maya approached, spotted Ziggy's state, then shared an exasperated look with me. "I think maybe she'd better call it a night."

"Call it a night?" Ziggy repeated through slurry spittle. "But we just started. We haven't even toasted yet, and that's my favorite part."

"I'd like to talk to Ziggy for a minute," I said to Maya.

"No way." Maya was already helping Ziggy to unsteady feet. "She's got to get back to her room and sleep this off. I have some stern words for her as well."

"Do you need some help?" I asked.

"Nope." Maya hefted Ziggy's arm over her neck to support her and began shuffling the gangly woman toward the exit.

Heavenleigh appeared next to me. "Is Ziggy okay?"

"Maya says she just needs to sleep it off."

"Does she need any help? I need to get away from

Clover. She keeps going on and on about investing in her kombucha company."

I followed Heavenleigh's gaze to the corner of the room. Clover had found a new target—one of Jennifer's aunties guessing by the beige palette—and was deep into her pitch.

The tinkling of glass at the head table caught our attention.

"Gotta go," Heavenleigh whispered. "Maid of Honor speech."

I weaved my way to the back of the room with the rest of the caterers to restock as Kismet took the microphone.

"Thank you all so much for coming tonight. It truly is an honor to be standing before you as Maid of Honor for this blessed occasion. First, I want to thank Saffron for finally acknowledging who her best friend really is, but I guess fate played a small role in that." Kismet laughed one of those fake bubbly chortles devoid of real emotion.

I blinked. Murmurs ran through the crowded tables. Saffron had gone three shades paler, as had Kismet's husband.

"And I especially want to thank Charmaine, may she forever rest in peace, for all the years of friendship and camaraderie. It *really* is a shame she can't be with us today."

A few faint claps followed, but quickly died down as Kismet continued.

"I want to start off with a story from our childhood at Bliss Ridge. Picture little Saffron and me playing in the mud by the chicken coop. Those were the days, right

Saffy?"

Saffron gulped and gave Kismet a weak smile.

"Poppy?" Angie popped up next to me. "I need you on champagne. Some of the glasses need filling before this speech is over. Look around and pour, pour, pour."

Thankfully, the rest of Kismet's speech ran according to tradition. A few jokes, childhood stories, and loving and congratulatory words of well-wishes. Crisis averted, and all glasses were filled in time for the toast.

Our slapdash catering crew made it through the rest of the evening without too many hitches. Lily and Greta had one minor tiff, the damaged contained to one tray of stuffed mushrooms that unfortunately took the brunt of their fury. Otherwise, it went about as well as possible, all things considered.

"Phew." Angie let out an enormous breath as the last of the guests slowly meandered through the exit doors. "We made it."

"Not bad for a big event, dearies," Shelby said. "I expect the wedding reception will go just as smoothly."

"How do the tips look?" Harper asked.

Shelby pulled a wad of bills from her pocket and began riffling through them. "Looks like you'll each get about a hundred bucks."

"Not bad," Greta said. "Decent haul for a few hours work."

Lily was less pleased. "That's it?"

"What's wrong, Lily?" Harper asked. "You too good for a little hard work?"

"That's enough," I said. "Let's clear this place up."

We rounded up the dishes, glasses, and utensils, leaving them in a big tub at the back catering table. It looked like a nightmare to wash.

"Don't worry, dearie," Shelby said. "These'll go in my industrial dishwasher at the diner. They'll be sparkling again in no time."

Mason's gloomy face turned even more glum. I supposed the dishwasher wouldn't load itself.

After closing down the community center, only Harper, Angie, Greta and I lingered behind, moving slowly at the late hour. Lily had had enough and departed for the Pearl as soon as she was released from duty.

"I'm wiped." Angie dropped onto a nearby bench. "I never stay up this late. I could fall asleep right here."

"Don't look now," Harper said. "Lovie alert at twelve o'clock."

"Too late," I said. "She's spotted us."

Lovie bustled up the path to meet us. "Good evening, ladies. What a nice night for a stroll."

Harper raised a skeptical eyebrow. "Bit late for prowling around town, isn't it?"

"The cool air is good for my skin. Anyway, I'm glad I caught up to you so I could warn you."

"Warn us about what?" I asked.

Lovie filled her lungs. "Well, I was having breakfast with Bev Trotter at the Waffle Jamboree in Vista this morning, and she ordered the rootie-tootie waffle tower and I got the Southern-style eggs benedict, which was overcooked, in case you were wondering, and Bev said her sister's friend's dog walker was out for a long walk with her prize-winning Weimaraners when she discovered a demonic altar with crystals and all kinds of wicked things in a clearing in the woods by the old saw mill off the Coastal Road."

Angie sat up straight. "Demonic?"

Harper scoffed. "How would she know what a demonic altar looks like?"

Greta squeezed forward. "What's a rootie-tootie waffle tower?"

Lovie held up her hands as if overwhelmed by all the questions, but I knew better. She was soaking in every second of this attention.

"You can't expect us to believe all this," I said. "A demonic altar at the old saw mill? Sounds like the title of a pulp mystery novel."

"I'm sharing as a *warning*," Lovie said. "Who knows what kind of ruffians are skulking about? They could be watching us from the woods right now."

Angie gasped and scanned the thick forest at the end of Main Street.

"Relax, Angie," Harper said. "No one is going to jump out of the forest. Lovie's just spreading gossip."

"I most certainly am not," Lovie protested. "And if you don't want to hear my warning, then I won't bother sharing with you ever again."

"Promise?" Harper smiled smugly.

Lovie pursed her lips.

"Can we go back to the rootie-tootie waffle tower?" Greta asked. "That sounded more interesting."

"No," Lovie replied with a huff. Then she turned heel and stomped off into the night.

"Demonic altars," Harper mumbled. "What a joke. That woman will believe anything."

"Actually," I said, "I think she may be right." Harper moved to protest, but I held up a hand to stop her. "Partially right. Lovie mentioned crystals and an altar. Kismet told me Saffron left the house the night of Charmaine's murder to conduct a secret ritual. Candles, trinkets, *crystals*, all that. And Greta and I found a crystal under Saffron's bed earlier."

Angie gave me a worried look. "Why would Saffron build a demonic altar in the woods?"

"The demonic part has Lovie's gossipy embellishment written all over it. Probably just a few sticks and twigs, but I want to check it out."

Harper waved a hand toward the church across the street. "I thought we were going to scope out the treasure tomb tonight?"

"We'll have time for that, too, but this altar could be a really important clue to finding out who killed my guest, so we should investigate."

Angie almost choked. "Right now? But the woods are dark and it's late and I'm half asleep already."

I nodded decisively. "Right now."

***

It took much convincing to get Greta to stay behind. No matter how much she told me the foil covering her ankle monitor would "confuse their radar array," I wasn't going to let her traipse into the woods and chance Deputy Todd stumbling upon us. She finally relented and headed back to the Pearl, where I told her to keep an eye on Ziggy and the others.

"The saw mill isn't far," Harper said. "Maybe a fifteen-minute walk. I think I know the clearing Lovie was talking about, too."

Angie clung to Harper the entire walk, which made for an awkward pace owing to Harper's exceptionally long legs and Angie's abnormally short ones.

"I hate these woods at night," Angie said. "They're so spooky."

"Don't worry," I said. "We'll protect you."

"What if we run into those Gold Hand people again? They almost caught us in the forest last time."

"They have no reason to be at the saw mill," I said. "Plus, despite what Greta thinks, we've seen nothing of them since Everett Goodwin left his cryptic message at the Pearl."

"That only makes me worry more," Angie said. "We don't know what they're up to. It could be anything. What if it's *their* demonic altar at the saw mill?"

"You really need to chill out," Harper said. "Nothing out here is going to—"

An owl hooted from a nearby tree.

Angie ducked under Harper's arm.

"Get out of my armpit. It was just an owl. This is it." Harper pointed at a building in the distance.

The bright waning moon and young trees cast long shadows over the cleared dirt road leading to the mill. The saw mill itself was a mish-mash of sea-rusted corrugated metal and weathered redwood planks. The glass had been broken out of two side windows, and nature had begun to overtake the leveled clearance around the structure.

"There's a little meadow off that way." Harper pointed toward a small path that led through a mess of branches into the deeper forest.

"I don't want to go in there," Angie said. "This place is already scary enough without demons."

"Look, Angie," I said, "I'm almost certain that whatever Bev's cousin's husband's coworker's imaginary friend saw was Saffron's little walkabout ritual. And I find it hard to believe that airy-fairy Saffron is dabbling in demons."

Harper peeled Angie off her arm and maneuvered her between us. "Poppy and I will sandwich you, okay? Nothing can hurt you."

Angie nodded but the fear in her eyes didn't dissipate.

We trudged through the branches along the narrow trail. Leading the way, I pushed the limbs out of our way and snapped those that would not give. It wasn't far before we opened into a clearing. The small meadow in the midst of the tall forest trees allowed full view of the night sky and constellations above. With no city lights to drown them out, the stars put on a dazzling show, even with the nearly full moon shining brightly. We stared upward for a few moments, enjoying the view. Waves crashed along the rocky shore somewhere in the distance.

"It's beautiful," Angie said.

Harper nudged Angie. "Not so scary anymore, huh?"

Angie smiled. "Now I remember why I love this place so much."

"Hey look." Harper pointed at a spot in the meadow. "That must be the altar."

We peeled our eyes from the sky and followed Harper's direction. A small pile of rocks had been gathered and three sticks poked straight up from between them.

"That's it?" Disappointment hung on my face.

"Did you expect more from Lovie?" Harper asked. "You said yourself it would probably be a bunch of sticks and twigs. I guess you weren't far off."

Angie stepped closer. "There's something wedged

between those rocks."

I knelt down for a better look. A slip of paper had been left weighted down by two of the stones. I carefully removed the rocks and held it up. "It's a tarot card."

"And this." Harper plucked a small pink-tinged rock from the very top of the altar and held it up for us to see.

"That's the same type of crystal Greta and I found under Saffron's bed." I held the card in both hands, studying the image by moonlight. A weather-beaten skeleton draped in gauzy rags sat atop a craggy rock. Across his lap lay a long scythe. Below the image read the name of the card: Death.

"I don't know anything about tarot cards," Angie said, "but I don't like the look of that one. And I don't think they're supposed to be left lying around. Wouldn't that ruin the deck?"

Harper shrugged. "I don't know either. Bunch of mumbo-jumbo, if you ask me."

"The Death card seems ominous." I pocketed the tarot card and crystal. "Maybe we can ask someone what it means, but that person isn't out here." I gave the clearing and the sky one last appreciative look. "Let's head back."

We returned through the brush to the saw mill and the dirt road beyond.

"Why was Saffron way out here, anyway?" Harper asked. "I get that she needed to perform some ritual, but why here?"

"I have no idea."

"It was really pretty," Angie said. "The clearing with the stars and everything. If I was going to perform a demonic ritual, that's where I'd do it."

After a few minutes of walking, we hit the main road

and followed it back. The moon was bright and lit our way, even through the tall redwoods towering above.

Harper and Angie were deep in conversation about the merits of hot chocolate versus chai when we finally made it into town. We turned a corner onto Main Street just as a car rumbled by at a glacial pace. As it passed, Deputy Todd's scowling visage peered from the driver's seat. He slowed to a stop and rolled down the window. "Out cruising the town, Miss Lewis?"

Harper spoke up, "It's called going for a walk, deputy. Nothing to see here. Continue your patrol. I'm sure there's some trouble-making roughneck just around the corner waiting for you to nab him."

Deputy Todd's scowl deepened. "Your sarcasm will get you into trouble one day, Miss Tillman. Mark my words."

Harper rolled her eyes. "Consider them marked." She waved her hands as if shooing him away.

After sparing a glare for Harper and me, he rolled up the window and drove on.

Harper waved at his taillights. "I'm going to report him to Mayor Dewey for harassing law-abiding citizens."

I huddled with Harper and Angie. "If Deputy Todd is on the prowl, we should hold off on searching the church."

Angie let out a relieved sigh. "Thank goodness."

Harper seemed dejected, but ultimately understood. "Another time," she said with a nod.

As we made our way further down the street and approached the bookstore, I spotted a truck parked out front. "Benjamin must be working."

"Benjamin, huh?" Harper smirked. "First-name basis

already?"

"Bit late to be working," Angie said.

I checked my phone. It was almost midnight. Angie would turn into a pumpkin any second, and Harper was fading, too. No time to stop and say hello.

I slowed my pace, secretly hoping Benjamin would exit, and we'd run into one another once again. Maybe share a few words, some witty banter. But as we passed, the door remained firmly shut. Paper was still plastered over all the windows, keeping whatever was going on inside a secret for now.

Nine

I FUMBLED FOR a mug from the upper kitchen cabinet the following morning.

"Shouldn't have stayed out so late." Greta perched haughtily on her stool and stirred a bowl of batter at the counter.

"It wasn't that late."

"You woke me up." Lily sat in her usual spot at the small kitchen table, sipping her tea.

"Still scared of the coffee machine?"

Lily took a long drink from her teacup. "I'm growing quite fond of tea, thank you very much."

"Sure, sure." I turned to Greta and peered into the bowl. Red and blue flecks speckled the batter mix. "What are you making?"

Greta grunted. "Rootie-tootie waffle towers."

"I thought you didn't know what they were?"

"Since when has that ever stopped me?"

I shrugged. She wasn't wrong.

Lily continued sipping her tea. "I ran into that

handsome bookstore owner on my way back last night."

My head shot up.

"I think he thought I was you."

I tucked a loose strand of my hair casually behind my ear. "Oh? Why's that?"

"He called me Poppy."

"What did you say to him?"

"I told him I wasn't Poppy."

"What did he say then?"

Lily raised an eyebrow. "You seem awfully interested in our small talk."

"Me? No I'm not."

"Well," Lily said, "it doesn't matter. There was no conversation. I was too tired and just wanted to get home to my bed."

"*My* bed, you mean."

Lily sighed. "Yes, yes."

"You never finished telling me what was going on with your collection," I said.

Her eyes darted toward Greta. "We can talk later."

"Greta," I said, "would you excuse yourself for a minute."

"Why?" Greta protested. "I didn't fart."

"No, I meant, could you give Lily and I some privacy?"

Greta eyed the bowl of batter with longing then plopped her whisk into the bowl and hopped off her stool. "Suit yourself. Batter needs to rest anyway."

Once alone, I turned back to Lily. "Go ahead."

Lily clutched her mug with both hands. "As you know, my collection will be released soon. I'm quite confident it will be successful—they always are."

"Go on," I said flatly, unwilling to stroke her ego.

"It's important that the collection do well. That's what I meant to say. You see, all those experimental treatments for my cancer were costly. Very costly. My finances are…lacking."

"You're broke?" The words choked their way out.

"'Broke' is such a harsh word."

"What about your condo remodel? Is that even real or have you been staying here under false pretenses?"

"That brings me back to the collection. You see, in order for the renovations to be completed, I need my collection to release. The sales will come in, as they always do, and things will be right as rain."

"I can't believe you've been keeping this from me. I've put myself out so you could stay here, and I feel like I've been lied to." My jaw clenched. "I've been rooming with Greta for you."

"And I do appreciate it. You've always been so hospitable. You make an excellent bed-and-breakfast hostess."

"I am not *your* hostess. You are not one of my guests."

Lily shrugged. "I don't know what you expect me to do about it. You can't expect me to live in a construction zone."

My mind immediately returned to the days I'd lived rough during my own renovations of the Pearl. While unpleasant, it wasn't impossible.

Lily spread her hands as if there were nothing else she could possibly do. "I know I've probably overstayed my welcome, but I just don't see what can be done about it."

Without hesitation, I strode to Greta's bowl of batter, plucked out the whisk and shoved it into Lily's open hand. "For starters, you can help Greta with breakfast. Don't bother protesting. You've done it before and nothing blew up. So, no more lolling around in the mornings, sipping tea and perusing the newspaper, acting like you're one of my paying guests. From now on, you can work for your room and board."

Lily gaped, alternating her gaze between the dripping whisk and me. "But I don't know how to make rootie-tootie waffle towers."

***

Post-breakfast, I set Greta to show Lily how to service the rooms. Despite her initial protests, Lily quickly fell in line after a few subtle threats of expulsion. And with the two of them set to task, I was freed up to take care of some other chores, mainly cleaning the porch and disposing of the small mountain of cigarette butts that had accumulated on the decking.

As I rounded the corner of the wrap-around porch, I found Maya legs splayed atop a yoga mat, holding her arms straight to the sky. She was facing away from me, toward the ocean, where the sound of the waves beating against the rocks drifted up the cliff.

"Good morning, doctor," I said.

Maya didn't move a muscle.

I admired her poise, wishing I had the same balance and level of serenity. "Maya?"

She let out a deep breath, righted herself, then turned her head. "Hi Poppy. How are you?"

"I'm fine, just doing a bit of cleaning up. How's

yoga?"

"Rejuvenating." She bent forward into Downward-facing Dog. "I thought a little digestive yoga would be fitting after that breakfast of... What did Greta call it?"

"Rootie-tootie waffle towers."

"Right. After all those waffles. You should join me."

I gave my broom one look then set it aside. Cleaning could wait. Digestive yoga sounded important. Good for me, even. I was doing myself a favor.

"Let's move into *Uttanasana*, or Standing Forward Bend." Maya walked her hands toward her feet, still bent over, and grasped her ankles.

I copied her pose as best I could, marveling at her flexibility, and ended up grabbing the back of my knees instead.

"I wish Saffron would have joined me," Maya said. "She would benefit from these poses."

"Why's that?" I huffed the words, breathless from being bent over.

"I'm sure you heard that she fainted yesterday."

"Uh-huh."

"Yoga provides relaxation, rejuvenation. My mother taught me that it's an excellent de-stressor. Now let's move into Warrior One."

I followed suit, lining my feet up with Maya's and reached toward the sky.

"I think her nerves are getting the better of her."

"Oh?" It was all I could muster while trying to hold my arms upward. My leg muscles screamed.

"Maybe rooming with Charmaine was a recipe for disaster, although I can't think of a better option. Maybe the basement?" Maya let out a gentle laugh, still effortlessly holding her pose.

One hearty chuckle made it out, but I was out of breath.

"Now down to a Garland Squat." Maya squatted, butt nearly to the ground, without blinking an eye.

Anything with the word squat in it wasn't going to happen. Not today. "I need a minute."

"Of course," Maya said with a nod. "Take your time. Do what feels right."

What felt right was leaning against the porch wall and shaking out my wobbly legs.

Maya moved through her poses. Triangle, then Child pose. I almost joined back in then—Child pose looked relaxing, like a good back stretch—but then she moved to Bow pose and I checked right back out.

"How's Ziggy doing?" I asked. "She wasn't at breakfast."

Back arched, arms behind her grasping her ankles, Maya responded as though she wasn't bent like a pretzel. "She needs a good, long rest. And definitely no more alcohol. She clearly drinks for a reason and it's out of control. Join me for Corpse."

"Sorry?"

"Corpse pose. You can do this one." She unpretzeled herself and waved me to the floor beside her.

I figured since it involved laying flat and required no contortions, I could manage, so I laid down next to Maya. "What's the reason, do you think?"

"For Ziggy? Probably the same as the rest of us. Maybe we've just found different outlets. She doesn't look remotely like she used to. Lots of surgery. And I think it was all to look more like Charmaine. That's the worst part. Charmaine bullied her mercilessly."

"That's not the first time I've heard that," I said.

"Ziggy got the worst of it. She was an easy target. I can't imagine she made it out of that childhood unscathed."

"What about you? You seem unscathed."

Maya let out a deep breath. "Charmaine was cruel to us all. Maybe I just hide it better. Maybe the yoga keeps me grounded."

I let the conversation drop as we relaxed into Corpse pose, letting the gentle waves mark the rhythm of our breathing. Who could fault these women for seeking out relief from the walking trauma that was Charmaine? Whether through drink, or crystals, or yoga, they deserved to be free of it.

We lay there for a few minutes more, two Corpses enjoying the salty air, the waves, and the stillness of our breathing.

***

Later that morning, I swept the upstairs landing during my newly acquired free time. Guests darted about on their daily tasks preparing for the wedding. Kismet disappeared into the bathroom for a shower while Saffron and the rest of the women put together wedding favors in the common area downstairs.

Greta and Lily worked slowly together. I couldn't complain since I didn't have to do the work myself, but it meant that they were still servicing the last of the guest rooms late into the morning.

I peeked in on the room shared by Kismet and Jennifer just as Lily threw a pillow at Greta's face. From the mussiness of Lily's short hair, I surmised it wasn't the first pillow thrown today. "Everything all right in here?"

"Fine," they both said together.

"I hope you're cleaning the rooms and not making more of a mess."

Lily shoved a towel into a nearby rolling hamper. "If *this one* would stop criticizing, then we'd be done by now."

"Ho ho," Greta said. "And if *this one* wasn't such a snotty little princess, we'd have been done an hour ago."

"Well, if *this one* hadn't re-covered all the beds I'd changed—"

"Enough," I said. "Greta, cut her some slack. She's learning. Lily, don't be a snob."

"That's it?" Lily asked, incredulous. "That's all you've got? I've been toiling away up here with your domestic house witch, and you tell me to stop being a snob?"

"A little domestic work will do you good."

"You heard her," Greta said. "Now, get back to work before this domestic house witch shoves her broom where the sun don't shine."

Defeated, Lily returned plucking dirty towels from the floor with her thumb and forefinger and dropping them into the hamper.

I ignored their occasional sparring and snide remarks catapulted across the room like barbed word bombs. Something else had caught my attention. Kismet's phone lay on the nightstand, unguarded.

Curiosity got the better of me. I checked the door and heard the sound of the shower going strong from the bathroom off the landing. Then I clicked on the phone. No lock screen. Kismet should know better, but it meant I could finally find out who the gardener was. I checked her messages first. Gardener was the top contact. The first text made me blush, the second made my eyes go wide and close the phone entirely. Definitely *not* something you'd say to your gardener. It was clear Kismet was stepping out on her husband. And after seeing their dynamic at the rehearsal dinner last night, it was clear that Kismet wasn't exactly heartbroken over her husband's lost affections. So, what motive did that leave her when it came to Charmaine? Maid of Honor? Could that be enough to murder someone? I remembered it was Kismet who knew about Saffron's ritual. Kismet who knew Saffron would be away, leaving Charmaine alone.

"What are you doing?" Greta asked. "I thought we weren't supposed to snoop."

"I wasn't snooping."

"Then why are you all red?"

I touched a hand to my cheek. It was warm to the touch. Kismet's messages must have made me flush more than I'd thought. "I'm fine."

Jennifer appeared in the doorway. "Who's snooping?"

"Uh, nobody," I said. "We're just finishing in here. C'mon ladies, let's wrap it up." I herded Greta and Lily out the door while Jennifer stood aside.

She stopped me before I could leave. "Poppy, a word, please."

"Of course."

She lowered her voice. "Something of mine has gone missing from this room."

My throat caught. "Really? What?"

Jennifer side-eyed Greta. "My bracelet. Do you know anything about that?"

"The beige one? No, of course not, I assure you. But I'm sure it will turn up. I will double check with Greta and Lily to be sure."

"I'd appreciate it," Jennifer said. "I'm a very forgiving person, but I'd like it returned."

"I understand."

I scooted past Jennifer and found Greta on the landing. Checking that Jennifer couldn't hear, I leaned in and hissed, "Did you take Jennifer's bracelet?"

"What? That hideous brown thing? Why would I take something that ugly?"

"Yes or no," I demanded.

Greta planted her fists on her hips. "No. Maybe your broke sister took it. Did you ever consider that?"

My jaw dropped. "How do you know about Lily?"

She crossed her arms. "I tripped and my ear accidentally fell against the kitchen door."

I tsked. "Well, don't say anything to anyone. That wasn't meant for your clumsy ears."

"Suit yourself," Greta said. "But I'll be happy to get my room back."

"Me too."

As Greta tottered down the stairs, I wondered if what she said could be true. Lily was broke, and a few of my own things had gone missing, too. Just how bad was her situation? Bad enough to steal? I shook the thought out of my head. I refused to believe it, no matter how likely, probable, and feasible the idea actually was.

Ten

My lunch plan that day was a cinnamon roll at Angie's bakery, washed down with a steaming mug of coffee. It had been a full morning, so I slipped into the bakery past my usual mid-day check-in time.

Harper was already there, seated at the single small café table with Mayor Dewey curled up in her lap. An empty plate lay in front of her with only a few crumbs left. She stabbed a thin finger at one morsel, licked it off, then stabbed at the next crumb. "Look who decided to join us," she said as the door's bell announced my arrival.

"Sorry, I got held up by some sticky fingers."

"Oh no," Angie said. "I hope everything's okay."

"It's fine. Mostly dealing with Greta and Lily at each other's throats. Thankfully, I'd had a lovely yoga session with Maya right before, so that buffered my irritation."

"How nice," Angie said. "Would you like your usual? I just put a fresh pot of coffee on, too."

I slumped into the remaining café chair. "Yes, please. That sounds wonderful."

While I waited, I pulled the late-night tarot card from my pocket and gave it a closer look. Death stared back at me.

"Any news on the secret ritual?" Harper asked.

"I haven't had a chance, but I did find out about a secret affair."

Harper sat up and scooched forward. "No kidding?"

"Kismet."

Angie set a gooey hot cinnamon roll in front of me. "The second Maid of Honor?"

"Yep."

"I guess everyone's got secrets," Harper said. "Secret rituals, secret affairs."

Outside, a figure passed in front of the bakery window toward the door. I only got a glimpse of chestnut hair before Harper quickly brushed the crumbs from her shirt and sat up straight, still careful not to disturb Mayor Dewey. Charlie entered a moment later.

"Hello everyone," Charlie said with a smile. "I thought I might find you all here."

"Hi Charlie," Angie said. "What can I get you?"

"Two dozen of those powdered sugar cookies. How'd the catering gig go last night?"

"It was great," Harper said. "No sweat, easy-peasy."

"More like okay," Angie said. "Between the drunk bridesmaid and that Clover woman trying to sell her kombucha drink to every poor soul she could corner, it wasn't too bad."

Charlie chuckled and nodded knowingly. "She tried the same thing with me. A group of them came into the shop."

"That's right," I said. "I forgot they went shopping."

"Yeah," Charlie said. "Too bad they didn't buy anything."

That gave me pause. "I thought they did? One of them showed me what they bought."

Charlie mused on this, then shook her head. "I don't think so."

"Tall lady with wavy blonde hair?"

Charlie tapped a finger to her chin. "There were two like that, weren't there? But I'm pretty sure no one bought anything. They had a bunch of bags, so it was probably from another store." She pointed at the card laying on the table. "Is that a tarot card?"

"Yeah," I said. "Do you know anything about tarot?"

"I don't know it myself, but I like to have my tarot read."

Harper choked on her coffee. "You do?"

"Sure," Charlie said. "I love tarot and palm reading and all that. I usually stop at Madam Mystica's place in Vista whenever I'm in town. You should try it some time."

Harper scoffed, then caught herself. "Er, I didn't realize you were so, uh, spiritual."

"Not spiritual, *per se*, but Madam Mystica knew I'd be opening my shop. She told me the cards showed I would be starting a new venture soon and sure enough, a few months later, I bought the gift store."

"'A new venture' could mean a lot of things," I said.

Charlie winked. "Reading into it is part of the fun."

"Speaking of new ventures," Angie said looking out her window, "I think the new bookstore owner is headed this way."

Now it was my turn to preen. I brushed the crumbs

from my shirt and swished a mouthful of coffee around to clean out any pesky bits from my teeth.

The door swung open and four pairs of eyes stopped Benjamin in his tracks. "Hello," he said warily.

Angie shuffled from behind the counter, took Benjamin's hand, and shook it vigorously. "You must be Benjamin Locke. Gosh, you're tall. I'm Angie Owens, and I'm so glad to finally meet you. This is my bakery, so that makes us neighbors. Aren't you excited to open? I was so excited when I first opened. My first day was a big blur, I can hardly remember any of it. And Roy—that's my husband—thought I was going to have a heart attack since I was running around like a chicken with my head cut off. So much to do, so little time. Everyone clamoring and asking you questions left and right and it's such a wonderful feeling, right?"

"Uh, right." Benjamin gave her a warm smile. "Nice to meet you."

Harper waved from her seat. "I'm Harper Tillman. I push the mail through your mail slot, and I carry the mayor around."

"The mayor?" Benjamin asked.

Harper pointed to the cat snoring in her lap.

"That's the mayor?"

"Yep," Harper said. "Duly elected. Ninety-nine percent approval rating."

"Ninety-nine?" Angie gawped. "Who's the one percent?"

Harper shrugged. "Polling was confidential, but I can guess."

Charlie stepped forward and shook Benjamin's hand. "I'm Charlie Barba. I run the Treasures of the Coast gift shop along the Coastal Road just outside of town."

"Nice to meet you, too. I haven't made it out there yet, but now I will be sure to visit."

Harper's expression, neutral until now, suddenly changed to a frown.

"And Poppy, it's good to see you again." Benjamin smiled sheepishly. "I think I ran into your sister yesterday."

"That was Lily."

"I have to apologize. You look a lot alike."

I waved him off. "It happens. How's the bookstore coming along?"

He gave his head a single shake. "Still working on the interior. Not too long now."

"Did you come by for anything specific?" Angie asked.

He pointed toward the pastry case. "One of those delicious-looking bear claws, please."

Angie nabbed the largest bear claw in the case and handed it over. "On the house. Welcome to Starry Cove."

"Thanks. That's very kind of you."

Angie beamed.

"Well," he said, clearly uncomfortable with all the attention, "guess I'll head out." He managed a small wave and left the bakery with his complimentary bear claw.

As soon as the door closed behind him, Angie swung around. "He's so dreamy. Did you see those curls?"

"Uh, no," Harper said. "All I saw were his pathetic attempts at flirting."

"Be nice, Harper," Charlie said. "He was just being friendly."

Harper slunk into her chair.

"He wouldn't stop looking at Poppy." Angie covered her mouth and giggled. "Should Ryan be jealous?"

"No," I said firmly. "We have a date tomorrow night and I'm looking forward to it, thank you very much."

"Did that guy seem familiar to anyone else?" Harper asked. "I felt like I've met him before."

I sat up straight. "I got the same impression." I nodded to Charlie and Angie. "What about you two?"

"Yeah, now that you mention it." Angie scrunched her face. "But I would have remembered if he'd come into the bakery before."

Charlie frowned and shook her head. "He probably has one of those faces, or you ran into him in Vista years ago." She shook her bag of sugar cookies. "Anyway, I'm off. I'll see you later."

As Charlie left, Harper oozed into her chair with a heavy sigh.

"Are you all right?" I asked in jest. "Do you need resuscitation?"

Harper flicked a long finger toward the tarot card on the table. "Who would have thought Charlie would fall for this mumbo jumbo?"

"Mumbo jumbo or not," I said, "maybe this Madam Mystica can help us understand what the card means? So, who's up for a field trip to Vista?"

"I'm willing to see what this charlatan is all about," Harper said.

"I'm curious, too," Angie said.

"Great. My guests have their bachelorette party tonight at the Pearl, so we need to get back before then. I'm hoping for a smooth night, zero drama."

Harper snorted. "Sure. That seems likely."

***

We piled into my car and headed to Vista as soon as Angie closed the bakery mid-afternoon. As I pulled into the tiny strip mall parking lot, a neon palm flashing in one of the windows told me I was in the right place. It took me a second to realize Madam Mystica's Divination Den was in the same shopping center as Sneaky Pete's Spy Supply, a hole-in-the-wall shop owned by a high school friend of Angie's.

"I didn't know Pete was right next door," Angie said. "I'll have to pop in and say hello."

"Madam Mystica first," I said.

"Then you can tell Sneaky Pete what a joke she is."

The storefront was dark on the outside, except for the bright neon, and as I opened the door, a thick cloud of incense wafted past my face. We shuffled into the small, claustrophobic space, inching closer to one another, careful not to touch the walls, which were draped with heavy, burgundy velvet curtains.

"Oof." Harper waved a hand in front of her face. "Smells like a hippy's dorm room in here."

Angie coughed. "Bit thick on the patchouli."

The drapery lining the back wall fluttered, and a figure swathed in folds of billowy jewel-toned fabrics emerged, trinkets tinkling at her wrists, neck, and ankles. "Welcome," she said in a deep, melodious voice, "to Madam Mystica's Divination Den. I am Madam Mystica." She followed this with a dramatic bow, waving her arm so the fabric flowed in her wake. "You are here to have your fortunes told. This I can see in my mind's eye."

"Nope," Harper said.

I stepped forward. "Actually, we're here for these." I held out the tarot card and rose-tinted crystals. She took the card with fingers clad in a multitude of gold and silver rings. The crystals were left untouched.

She spent a moment examining the card. The only movement were her eyes, caked with what looked like three-days-worth of mascara and sparkling eye shadow in shades of purple and blue.

Finally, she handed the card back. "This is a tarot card. The Death card. I am not familiar with this particular deck."

"Yeesh," Harper said. "We *already* know it's the Death card."

I frowned at the mystic's ambiguity. "We were hoping you could tell us more about it."

The woman spread her arms wide. "The wisdom of Madam Mystica does not come without a price."

My eyes narrowed. "What price?"

"You are here to have your fortunes told, yes?"

"No," Harper repeated.

I shushed Harper with a stern look, then returned to Madam Mystica. "If we get our fortunes told you'll tell us about the card?"

Madam Mystica spread her arms wide again. "So I have foretold."

"Fine," Harper said. "I'll go first. This should be over real quick."

The woman eyed Harper up and down. A hint of a smile rose in one corner of her mouth and the light caught a sparkle in a glob of her eyeshadow. "Come with me." She waved Harper to a small round table in one corner covered in a sequined tablecloth. They took their respective seats and Madam Mystica shoved her hand across the table, palm up. "Give me your right hand, and I will tell you what you need to hear."

Harper lolled her head our way, gave us one of her signature eye rolls, then put out her hand.

The old woman snatched Harper's wrist with her bony fingers, then rubbed the top of Harper's hand with a surprisingly delicate touch. "Your skin is smooth. Long, thin fingers. You are curious, but easily frustrated."

"That's Harper all right," Angie whispered next to me.

Madam Mystica next turned the hand palm-side up. The charms and bells on her bracelets jingled as she ran her forefinger along the ridges and valleys of Harper's palm. An occasional grunt or peep of surprise were the only sounds other than our breathing. "I see that you are a reluctant leader of great wit." Her cakey eyes met Harper's. "But little charm."

Harper frowned. "Little charm? What's that supposed to mean?"

Harper's questions were ignored as Madam Mystica returned her focus to the palm. "Now to your destiny." She ran a finger along the creases and lines. "You are passionate about those you love."

My friend squirmed in her chair.

The woman closed her eyes and reached her free hand out into ethereal air. "You are in a state of love now. I see it in my mind's eye."

Harper turned sheepish and tried to pull her hand back, but Madam Mystica clutched her wrist like a vise.

Angie grabbed my arm and wriggled it. "She must be talking about Charlie."

Leaning in closer, Madam Mystica squinted at Harper's palm. "Ah-ha. This is interesting."

"What?" Harper scooched forward. "What is it? Do you see someone?"

"You will surprise yourself and others."

"How?" Harper asked with urgency.

The old woman's eyes closed once more and her head drifted side to side as she began a rhythmless humming. A moment of this droning and she suddenly stopped. "Yes, yes. I see it."

"You see her?" Harper could barely contain her excitement.

"I see no her. You will do something selfless. Utterly selfless."

"Oh," Angie said. "That doesn't sound like Harper at all."

I snorted quietly. "Definitely not."

Harper glared our way. "Would you two quiet down? I'm trying to listen to my destiny here."

The old woman tossed Harper's hand back her way and put a finger to her temple. "That is all I can see."

"That's it?" Harper stared at her own palm. "There's nothing more you can tell me? What about Charlie? I need to know what happens with me and Charlie."

But Madam Mystica only waved Harper off, ending their session.

Harper shuffled from the table and joined Angie and me.

Angie put a hand on Harper's back and gave her a gentle hug. "It's okay, Harper. I'm sure Charlie loves you too."

My friend seemed dejected, shoulders slumped, eyes

cast down rubbing at her palm of destiny. "Angie's right," I said. "You'll see."

"I will read the short one next." Madam Mystica beckoned toward Angie with a single finger.

Angie turned her large blue eyes to Harper and me, then gulped and made her way to the small table. She gingerly scooted into the chair opposite the medium.

"For you, the divination orb."

"Not the palms?" Angie held out her hands.

Madam Mystica eyed Angie's pudgy palms and shook her head. She reached under the table and, heaving with both hands, pulled up a pearly, translucent globe the size of a soccer ball and set it in the middle of the table. "The divination orb."

Angie's eyes widened. "It's so pretty."

"You will place your hands upon the divination orb and I will divulge your true destiny."

Angie glanced at us with excitement on her face, then slowly and carefully placed both palms against the smooth glass ball, stout fingers stretched wide.

Madam Mystica inhaled deeply, closed her eyes, and began to wind her hands around the globe in figure eights. "It is coming to me slowly," she said. "It is difficult to make out, obscured by an impenetrable white cloud."

"Flour," Harper whispered from the corner of her mouth.

"There," Madam Mystica said breathlessly. "I see you now. You are wielding a..." The lines around her eyes deepened as she pinched them tighter. "A thick wooden baton."

Angie gasped. "My rolling pin!" In her excitement, Angie leaned forward and lost her balance on the chair, but she steadied herself with one hand on the table.

"Hands on the orb," Madam Mystica said flatly.

Angie quickly readjusted and placed her palm back onto the orb's surface.

The old woman began to hum and wind her hands around the orb again. "I see…something you make will be enjoyed by a surprising party."

"A surprising party," Angie repeated. "A food critic? Is it Marissa Wyszynski from *Baker's Treat Magazine*? I heard she'd be visiting this region, but I thought it might be next month or the month after. Maybe it's this month. I can't remember. What can you see? What can you see?"

Again, Madam Mystica put a hand to her temple. "I can see no more."

Angie, eyes somewhat wild now, leaned as far over the table as her short stature would allow. "You have to tell me if it's Marissa Wyszynski!"

Madam Mystica dismissed Angie's demands with a wave of her adorned hands. "No more."

"C'mon, Angie." Harper pulled her away from the table. "I'm sure Marissa Wyszynski will love your baking."

That meant it was my turn next. I sidled into the chair vacated by Angie. The divination orb had disappeared, replaced by a deck of cards. Tarot cards.

Madam Mystica grinned up at me. "For you, the Tarot."

"I'm ready," I said with a shaky voice.

She shuffled the cards with deft fingers. "The cards never lie." Slowly, and with great dramatic effect, she split the deck and turned over the top card, laying it on the table for all to see.

A shiny golden chalice floated in the center, filled and overflowing with shimmering streams of water. The name at the bottom of the card shone as the faint light of the room cast over the golden letters. Ace of Cups, it read.

Madam Mystica stared at the card, then let out a low hum. "The Ace of Cups can mean many things. New relationships." Her thickly mascaraed eyes flicked up at mine. "Perhaps a new beau?"

I tried hard to keep from reacting. *A new beau?*

"Perhaps," Madam Mystica continued, "the strengthening of an existing relationship." Her eyes caught mine again, and she raised a darkly defined eyebrow. "Only you can know."

Old relationship or new? Ryan or Benjamin. I fought down a flush at my cheeks.

"Now," Madam Mystica said, "show me your card again."

I fished the Death card from my pocket and handed it over.

The old woman studied the card with more scrutiny this time. "Tell me where you found this."

"In a clearing in the woods, tucked between stones at a little makeshift altar along with this." I pulled out the rosy crystal and set it on the table.

Madam Mystica sneered at the stone, then returned her attention to the card. She turned it over in her hand, examining the back, then ran a bony finger along the straight edge. "What else can you tell me?"

"We think it was left there by a young bride-to-be."

Madam Mystica squinted one eye at me as if she knew I was holding back.

"And that there was a murder at my bed-and-breakfast the other night and she might be a suspect. I found another of those crystals under her bed."

She lay the card on the table in front of her and tapped at the weathered skeleton figure. "This was found in the woods?"

I nodded.

"Mm-hmm."

"Well?" I asked after a moment of silence passed.

"The card itself could mean a number of things. That is the nature of the Tarot. It can be taken literally, as death, but more often it is figurative. The death or end of something. Sometimes new beginnings, new life."

"That's a bit of a swing, isn't it?" Harper asked. "Life *or* death. Really clears it up."

Madam Mystica smiled and spread her hands. "It is the Tarot. I would suggest you ask this young woman what was in her heart."

I stared at the card on the table. "Can you tell us why it may have been left behind?"

"A sacrifice—"

Angie gasped and clutched at her collar.

"To ensure the cards' intent comes to pass," the mystic continued.

"What about the crystals?" I asked. "There was one found with the card, obviously left there on purpose. Are they another sacrifice?"

Madam Mystica let out a flippant scoff. "Do I look like a gem trader to you? Crystals are a scam." She waved dismissively at the crystals on the table. "Just cheap trickery meant to part fools with their money." She eased herself from her chair, leaning heavily on the table. The trinkets at her wrists jangled as she slowly straightened her back, letting loose a mighty crack. "Now," she said, "that will be one hundred and fifty dollars."

Eleven

IT WAS ALREADY early evening when I returned to the Pearl, fresh from Madam Mystica's ominous prognosticating. Greta stood atop her stool, washing a pile of dirty dishes. Voices and laughter of the women carried from the common area where they gathered for Saffron's bachelorette party.

"Took long enough," Greta said.

I slipped my apron on and quickly washed my hands. "Sorry, we ran into an unexpected delay. What can I help with?"

"Nothing now. I set out the cheese plate and tea like we discussed and left them to their own devices. They've been clucking like chickens for the past hour, Saffron's cried three times, and Zippy has a flask hidden in her back pocket."

"It's Ziggy, and how do you know that?"

Greta stared up at me with a glimmer in her eye. "I wasn't born yesterday, and I know my flasks."

I didn't like the idea of Ziggy drinking, but at least

she was in a safe place, unsolved murder aside, and surrounded by friends. Plus, Maya was there, and I was sure she'd have an eye on Ziggy.

"Some fella came by earlier looking for you."

"Really?" My voice held more excitement than I wanted to give away.

Greta scowled at me. "It wasn't Ryan."

"Who was it then?" I asked innocently.

She continued to glare. "Said his name was Benjamin. Complimented the house. Said he loved old houses."

"Oh? That's the new bookstore owner." I struggled to keep the delighted flutter out of my voice.

Suddenly, my phone exploded with vibrating and dinging notifications. "What the…" I pulled it from my pocket. My body slumped. "It's the Smarty Pants app. It says the front door lock has malfunctioned. And this other notification says the kitchen door has malfunctioned, too."

"Huh." Greta continued washing dishes.

I tried the kitchen door, but the existing lock had been integrated into the Smarty Pants mechanism and wouldn't budge. I knelt down and inspected the lock. Deep scarring marred the device, and the part had clearly been tampered with. My eyes narrowed. "Do you happen to know anything about this?"

"Hmm?" She continued scrubbing.

A few long strides took me from the kitchen into the foyer and I inspected the front door, where I found similar damage.

Saffron must have spotted me from the common room. She called out, "Is everything okay?"

"Just a minor malfunction," I said.

"What kind of malfunction?" Kismet asked.

I groaned inside. The scuffs had Greta's fingerprints all over them. "The doors are having a little trouble opening, nothing to worry about." I raised my voice for the next part to make sure the old woman heard me. "Greta is already working to fix them."

Jennifer rose from her chair. "Are you saying we're locked in here?"

Trying to ease any raising fears, I held up my hands. "We're working on the problem right now and it shouldn't take too long to get it straightened out."

"But we can't get out?" Jennifer's face had gone a few shades beiger.

Saffron, who sat on the floor nearby, tugged at Jennifer's pants. "What's the big deal? Were you planning on leaving?"

"No, of course not." Jennifer sat back down.

I put on my best hostess smile. "We'll have it fixed in no time. Carry on."

I turned heel and stormed into the kitchen, my smile erased at the sight of my housekeeper scrubbing and humming from atop her little stool.

"Oof," she said. "Lots of dishes tonight."

"Tell me what you did," I demanded. "Then you'll be spending the rest of your time fixing it."

"Eh?"

"I found that toothpick you shoved into the coffee machine this morning, so I know you sabotaged the doors, too."

Greta stopped and turned. "I certainly did not."

"Then explain the malfunctioning to me. Explain the scratches."

The tiny woman folded her arms in defiance. "Can't trust 'em."

"What does that even mean?"

"It was communicating with my tracking device."

I rubbed at my temple. "You sabotaged the doors and the coffee machine because you thought they were communicating with your ankle monitor? And now we're trapped in this house because the locks are stuck. Wonderful."

"You're welcome."

A woesome wail came from the common room, and Greta and I poked our heads through the swivel kitchen door that looked onto the women through the dining room.

Ziggy sat on the floor, slumped against the sofa with her head resting in Maya's lap. She gripped a silver flask in one hand and tears streamed down her face, marking wet spots on Maya's gray yoga pants. "I really love all you girls," Ziggy slurred through sobs, "I'll be so sad when this is over."

"There, there," Maya said, patting Ziggy on the head. With the other hand, she attempted to reach down and take the flask, but Ziggy pulled it out of reach.

Clover placed a hand on Ziggy's shoulder. "Maybe you should drink kombucha instead of wine, Zigs."

Kismet took a swig of wine from an oversized goblet. "Give it a rest, Clover. Every other word out of your mouth is kombucha. We're sick of it."

"It was just a suggestion," Clover said with a snip in her voice. "You don't have to be rude."

Heavenleigh let out a deep sigh. "The kombucha thing *is* growing tiresome. I don't know about the rest of you, but I've had my fill."

Clover glanced quickly at each woman, checking their reactions. When no one came to her defense, she stood straight up. "I thought I could count on the support of my friends. This business is my life, and I have poured everything into it."

Kismet rolled her eyes. "Oh, for the love of…"

"No one is attacking your business, Clover," Maya said. "We support you, but kombucha isn't always the answer."

Clover turned on Maya. "And I suppose yoga is?"

"I didn't say that. Although a few deep breaths couldn't hurt."

"Well, maybe my kombucha could help right now. More wine for Ziggy definitely isn't the answer."

Ziggy wailed again and dropped her forehead onto Maya's leg.

"Can we all get along, please?" Saffron's delicate voice barely cut through the tension. "I just want to spend a night celebrating with my closest girlfriends."

"Why am I here, then?" Heavenleigh asked under her breath.

"Or me?" Jennifer added.

That was when Saffron lost it. After glancing at her future sister-in-law and her childhood friend, she too, burst into tears, joining Ziggy in the sorority of sobbing.

Greta, whose head poked through the door directly below mine, whispered, "This is the worst bachelorette party I've ever snooped on. I hoped there'd at least be strippers."

Despite the sobbing going on around her, Kismet appeared unfazed. She gestured at Maya with her wine goblet. "Maybe you should prescribe Saffron and Ziggy something for their nerves?"

Maya shook her head emphatically. "No way."

Clover stood up. "Well, I'm going to get some kombucha for them. My Kalm Kombucha should do the trick." She turned heel and headed toward the kitchen as the others let out a collective groan.

Greta and I pulled our heads in before she could spot us. Greta scurried atop her stool to the dishes and I picked up a tea towel and casually began drying. A moment later Clover pushed through the swivel door, pulled open the fridge, and grabbed as many Kalm Kombuchas as she could carry.

"Do you need any help?" I asked. "That's quite an armful."

"I've got it, thanks." She fumbled with the bottles but ultimately secured them in her arms.

"How's the business going?" I asked. "Have you sold any around town?"

"Your general store bought a case, so that's a start." She stared at the bottles wistfully. "Just not enough."

"So, it's *not* going well?"

Clover sagged. "To be honest, no. I need more funding. Unless I sell a truckload of these, I could be in trouble."

"I thought Charmaine was your funding."

"Charmaine isn't funding anything now."

"Good point."

"I'm only pushing hard because I need to make sure the company survives without her backing. I've approached Heavenleigh to see if she and her father are interested in investing."

"Why Heavenleigh?" I asked.

"Her family's got a bunch of money."

"I thought her dad ran the commune?"

"He does," Clover said. "That means they have all the money. I held off for a while since I saw Charmaine and Heavenleigh talking that first day we arrived and obviously that would have been awkward. I couldn't exactly ask Heavenleigh to invest with Charmaine standing right there. They were in a pretty heated conversation, so I didn't want to intrude. But now I'm wondering if Charmaine said something to her about the company, or if Heavenleigh's soured on the business with all my pushing and prodding. I was confident she'd jump at the opportunity. Now, I'm not sure."

"Oh, I don't know about that," I said with encouragement, although I *did* know about that since Heavenleigh had told me herself that she was wary of Clover's intentions.

She looked down at the bottles in her arms with a dejected frown. "You wouldn't possibly be interested in invest—"

"No," I said quickly. "And maybe you should play it cool for a while."

Her shoulder slumped. "I guess you're right. I should put these back."

I opened the fridge door, then help her return the bottles to the top shelf. "I'll make some fresh tea instead."

Once Clover swiveled through the kitchen door and returned to the other guests, Greta hopped off her stool. "Sounds like that kombucha's a bust."

"It's actually pretty good," I said. "It's running a business that's hard."

"Too bad her money train bit the big one."

"Right. Her money train…" It was clear that Clover needed financing for her business, so losing Charmaine would have been a massive hit. But she'd also hinted she was looking for investors *before* Charmaine had died. Was Clover on the hunt because she knew something? If she saw Heavenleigh and Papa Zamora has her *new* money train, then Charmaine wouldn't need to stick around. In fact, it may have been easier if she were out of the way entirely.

***

Each guest nursed a nasty hangover the next morning, but none more than Ziggy, bleary-eyed, frazzled, and far from the bright ray of energy she'd exhibited the first day.

Breakfast had been light, as appetites were low following a night of binging, and most guests left the table quickly to tend to their headaches and stomachs.

Only Saffron remained, not because she wasn't suffering. She held her head in her hands and groaned occasionally as I tidied up the table.

"Is everything okay?" I asked.

She pushed a sheet of paper away with a scoff of disgust. "There's still so much to do and the wedding is tomorrow."

I lay a hand on my back pocket where I'd stowed the tarot card and rose quartz for safe keeping. "Weddings are stressful. And losing your Maid of Honor… It's a lot to process."

She puffed out a breath. The hair falling in front of her eyes blew back then fell back into place. "Maybe this wedding is cursed."

I gripped the table. "Cursed?" I spat the word out in my haste. "What do you mean?"

She looked at me quizzically. "It's just a figure of speech, Poppy. Are you okay?"

"Sorry," I said, regaining my composure. "It's just that, um, I found some things that seemed odd."

"What things?"

I pulled out the tarot card and placed it on the table along with the crystals.

Saffron stared at the items in silence.

"Do you recognize these?"

For a moment she didn't move, then she started chewing on her bottom lip and nodded.

"You did more than just step out for some fresh air that night, didn't you?"

Saffron nodded.

"You went out to the forest—by that abandoned saw mill—and you...what? What exactly did you do?"

She didn't answer right away. Instead, she fidgeted with a long necklace dangling at her throat. A locket. With a fingernail, she clicked the locket opened and shared that it was a picture of her fiancé, Chad. "I went out there for him. For us, really."

"What do you mean?"

"I went out there to perform a ceremony. My maharishi swore that the Death card—for new beginnings—and my rose quartz crystals—for love—would ensure a happy marriage. Kids, love, all that. But it had to be performed in the woods at midnight and under a full moon. Those were the requirements. And that night was the full moon. It was my only opportunity." She reached out and lay a hand on my forearm. "Don't laugh."

"But why not just say so? Why keep it a secret?"

"I saw your face just now. You wanted to laugh. That's why. And then Charmaine happened. So you see, I couldn't just flip my story on its head. Besides, Chad's family already dislikes me."

I grimaced, remembering Mother Beige's less-than-kind take on Saffron eccentricities from a few days ago.

"I couldn't let Jennifer find out," she said. "It would get back to the family and that would make it worse for Chad and me. But I couldn't miss the full moon, so I snuck out early, and when I came back, you saw me and I didn't know what to say in that moment, so I lied." She closed the locket and held it tightly in her hands. "Maybe if I hadn't gone out, Charmaine wouldn't have…" Tears welled in her eyes.

It was my turn to lay a hand on her arm in comfort. "It's okay. You couldn't have known."

"And the sight of her laying there in a puddle of kombucha. Those horrible red marks on her neck." Saffron clutched at her own delicate neck, then her eyes widened. "You don't think that kombucha was poisoned, do you?"

"I don't know," I said. "Why would you think that?"

"It's just that Clover's been so uptight about her kombucha company. You've heard her go on and on. And according to Clover, Charmaine was a pretty loud silent partner."

"She did say Charmaine had been making things difficult."

"She *hated* giving in to Charmaine. Hated it. But you know Charmaine could be a real bully sometimes. Make you do things you don't want to do. She had a way about her."

"So I've heard."

"And that way was either her way *or else*."

***

I'd given the weary women a while to float downstairs after their post-breakfast respite. Some were sprightlier than others, but slowly, they made their way into the common room and got to work on frilly, lacy wedding favors under the supervision of Saffron, who led the task with gentle directives. Only Ziggy remained upstairs, yet again sleeping off the rest of a wicked hangover.

Earlier that morning I'd left a message for the Smarty Pants technician inquiring about any permanent damage caused by Greta's chaotic attempts to overthrow the system. While I waited for an answer, she and I got to work servicing the empty bedrooms.

"You should be thanking me," Greta said after I'd admonished her for the fifteenth time that morning. "That smart door has been nothing but trouble. Alert this, and alert that. Sends my blood pressure to the moon."

"You've sabotaged this entire house," I said. "I found the toothpick you shoved into the toaster's computer, too. In addition to the one that broke the coffeemaker."

"Hmph. I chose my weapon carefully."

I rounded on the old woman. "Do you know how much that's going to cost to fix?"

"No," Greta snapped back. "Maybe ask the toaster since it's so smart."

Heat rose in my cheeks. Before I growled something nasty at her, I decided the best thing to do was separate myself from the sight of her. "I'm going to work on the next suite. You can finish this one alone."

She whip-cracked a fresh pillowcase linen. "Suit yourself." Her tone was as sharp as mine.

"Don't sass, or I'll send Lily in to help you."

Greta's face scrunched like a prune.

I grumbled my way into Heavenleigh's and Maya's room, took one look around at the clothes hanging off chair backs, dishes accumulated on the bedside tables, and toiletries laid out in a dizzying mess, and sighed. The only way to tackle the mess was to start, so I began in one spot and worked clockwise, wiping down surfaces and throwing out bits of trash and used napkins.

Near a dresser along the far wall, I stooped down to pick up a discarded wine bottle. The ladies sure had ended the night hard, despite the tea I'd provided.

On my hands and knees, I reached for the bottle, but something else caught my eye. Shining specks lay on the floor shoved far against the wall under a dresser. The faint light from the window streamed in at just the right angle to glint off its surface, projecting a brilliant shade of green. I stretched my arm far under the dresser and pulled the shiny objects from their hiding spot.

When my fingers unfurled, my breath caught. I recognized the items immediately. They were the emerald earrings Charmaine wore the night she was murdered. There was no mistaking the deep, rich color. Charmaine had made a point to show them off to the others. But what were they doing here, hidden surreptitiously under a dresser in a dark corner? Perhaps Charmaine had removed the pieces, and someone took them later, placing them here where they thought no one would find them. There was another possibility, though, one that ran a shiver down my spine. Could these have been taken—no, ripped—from Charmaine as she was murdered, only to be stashed for safekeeping in this particular hiding spot? One thing was certain. This jewelry hadn't hidden itself. Someone had done this intentionally. And I'd bet that someone was a cold-blooded murderer.

Twelve

I RAPPED LIGHTLY on the door to the room shared by Clover and Ziggy. There had been no sign of Ziggy since her brief appearance at breakfast, so I assumed she was still sleeping it off, but I wanted to make sure she was okay.

After no response, I eased open the door and poked my head into the room. Sure enough, Ziggy was prostrate on the bed with her arms securing a pillow over her head.

"Go away, Clover," she said. "For the last time, I'm not interested."

"It's Poppy."

Ziggy flung the pillow off her head and sat up. "I'm so sorry, I thought you were Clover."

"Don't worry," I said with a laugh, "I'm not here to sell you kombucha."

"I wish it were only that. She's been trying to get me to invest. I think she's desperate now that Charmaine's gone. She keeps nagging me about it every second she can." Ziggy flopped her head back onto her pillow. "She's relentless."

"I came by to ask if you're feeling any better."

Ziggy put a hand to her temple. "Still have an awful headache. I think it's the same one I've had for days. Maya told me to drink more water."

I glanced toward a tray in the corner. Each room is supplied with a water carafe and glasses. A simple service, but one I find adds a bit of comfort and care to each room. I stepped to it now and poured Ziggy a glass of water.

"Thanks," she said, taking the cup. "I suppose I should listen to my doctor."

"Probably a good idea."

"Maya has a good bedside manner. She doesn't judge, either." Ziggy's eyes flicked up as though checking my reaction, but I remained serene. "It's not my fault, you know, the drinking. Maya says bullies can drive us to find coping mechanisms and mine is just more noticeable."

"Wise words."

"She reminded me that we were all Charmaine's victims, and it was okay to feel angry."

I thought of my own anger at times of betrayal and nodded. "I understand."

A knock at the door frame startled me.

Heavenleigh poked her head in. "How are you feeling, Zigs? We miss you downstairs. Saffron's asking for you."

Ziggy let out a heavy groan, still holding her head. "Tell her I'll be down in a few minutes."

"Okay, but don't take too long." The mock cheerfulness in Heavenleigh's voice was hard to miss. "We're about to start gluing baby's breath to some gaudy napkin rings, and I'm sure you don't want to let Saffron down." She turned and quickly disappeared down the stairs.

Another deep grumble oozed from Ziggy as she stared daggers at the spot where Heavenleigh had just been. "You know, that first day here, Heavenleigh and Charmaine were at it pretty thick."

"'At it'?" I repeated.

"Yeah. Charmaine would accost anyone—she had no fear. And she was laying into Heavenleigh pretty bad."

"What were they talking about?"

"Oh," Ziggy said with a scoff, "I have no idea. I couldn't hear them. Heavenleigh looked pretty scared, though. Like a scolded child. None of the rest of us would ever talk to Heavenleigh that way."

"Why not?"

"She's the golden child, Papa Zamora's baby girl. She was untouchable on the commune. I'm not saying she was a brat or anything, quite the opposite, but she's probably not used to having one of us shake a finger at her."

Through what appeared to be great effort, Ziggy flung her legs over the side of the bed and dropped her feet to the floor as though made of lead. She touched a hand to her temple again.

I grabbed her arm to steady her. "Are you all right?"

"My head is pounding like a snare drum."

"Maybe you should stay in bed."

"You heard what the golden child said. Saffron is waiting for me. Plus, I feel bad leaving them to do all the work." She leaned heavily against me as she tried to stand up.

"You're wobbling," I said.

"I might still be a tad drunk. Can you help me down

the stairs? I'm completely useless right now."

"Of course."

I led Ziggy from her room and slowly, inch-by-inch, we descended the stairwell to the common room. With each step, each tight clutching of my arm, it became clear that Ziggy was, in fact, useless. She could no more take care of herself than a milk-drunk newborn babe. In her perpetual intoxication, it would have been impossible for her to overtake a lioness like Charmaine and emerged unscathed, let alone the murderous victor.

***

Later that afternoon, I dragged Lily and Greta behind me and ran out the kitchen door. We were already late for the pre-wedding catering crew rehearsal, and if I knew my friend, she'd be steaming and stomping in General Angie mode.

"We won't get there any sooner if you break my arm." Lily pulled her arm away from my grasp.

"Sorry. It's just that—" I stopped at the sight of Daisy sniffing intently under a dense shrub.

"What?" Lily asked.

I pointed toward Daisy, where a collection of tan and white nubs had been piled and half-hidden from view. "What's that?"

Greta leaned down with a creaky groan, squinted, then let out a huff. "Yep, it's butts."

"Don't be so crude," Lily said.

"No, she's right." I gently pushed Daisy aside and stooped over the pile for a closer look. "It's cigarette butts. And there's something else here." I pinched a crumpled piece of paper from the ashy pile.

"Do we have time for this?" Lily asked. "I thought we were running late."

I ignored her and uncrumpled the note.

Dear Jen,

It would be a shame if your family were to find out about us. I haven't said anything yet, but if you insist on ignoring me, I won't have a choice.
With love, Char.

I couldn't believe what I was reading. I read it again, and then a third time. Were Charmine and Jennifer an item? It was almost impossible to reconcile beigey, bland Jennifer with chic Charmaine. With such little time, I hadn't grown to know Charmaine, but everything I'd learned told me this crumpled and discarded note was more a threat than a request. It was like a flashing marquee laying out a strong motive for Jennifer.

Lily swatted at my arm. "What could possibly be so interesting?"

"Nothing." My hand closed around the note, and I shoved it into my pocket. I gave the pile of cigarette butts a last glance and made an internal reminder to ask Jennifer a few pointed questions. "Let's go."

Angie met us at the door of her bakery, which she held open with one stubby foot and a sassy hip. "Hurry up you three. Harper's here already."

I gave her a stiff salute. "Yes, ma'am."

"Finally." Harper slumped against the wall nibbling the remnants of a cinnamon roll. "Angie's on the warpath."

Lily, Greta, and I ordered ourselves smartly next to Harper, one-by-one like a police lineup of miscreant caterers.

Angie smacked a spoon against her palm with a crack. "All right, listen up. Let's debrief from the rehearsal dinner. The wedding reception will be an even bigger party, so expect more demands on your time and attention. In addition to the picky mothers-in-law and finicky grandmothers, the real challenge will be the ubiquitous freeloaders lurking behind every gauzy drape and floral display. They want to lick your canapé tray clean, dual-fist champagne, and send you back for more before you can say 'hors d'oeuvres' three times fast."

Harper snorted. "Sounds like Greta."

"I'm not the one dual-fisting cinnamon rolls."

Harper choked on an inhaled crumb.

"Enough." Angie slapped the spoon against her palm and a deafening silence took over the bakery. "Right now, I have a platoon of undisciplined servers who need a good whack in the behind. These wedding guests will *eat you alive*."

Just as General Angie was about to dive into her demands of us, the bakery door shot open with the violent clang of the bell. It was Shelby, breath heaving, wide-eyed, beehive ragged and wobbling. "It's a nightmare, dearies."

Angie spun. "What is?"

Shelby's legs trembled as she lurched forward, and I rushed to grab a chair before she collapsed. "They're gone!"

"What's gone?"

"The appetizers, dearie. All the prepared food. All of

it is gone."

"What do you mean they're gone?" Angie's face was a mix of disbelief and horror. "I was over this morning while you and Mason were finishing up."

"Mason," Shelby growled. "That pimply nitwit left the back door open and Mayor Dewey and Daisy got in. Inhaled the whole lot like a pair of furry vacuums. Ravaged the place. There's nothing left, dearie." She dropped her head into her hands.

Angie's face went white. "But the wedding's tomorrow. We have nothing?"

"Just your cake, dearie."

Angie slumped into the remaining chair.

"What can we do?" I asked. "Can we remake everything?"

Shelby shook her head and Angie's eyes lolled as if dazed.

"Even if I raided the diner's fridge for supplies, there's just no time, dearie. We've been prepping for days already."

"What if you had extra hands?"

Lily's eyes narrowed to tiny slits.

"The four of us could help," I said.

Angie shook out of her daze. She held a hand out to Shelby. "It could work."

Harper stuttered. "Uh, I'm not exactly free."

Greta shook her ankle. "The government lackeys won't let me."

Lily placed a delicate hand to her chest. "Obviously, I have no experience in food preparation, so I'll have to pass as well."

I grabbed Angie's spoon and cracked it against my

palm. Eyes widened all around. "What's wrong with all of you? Angie and Shelby need our help. We can give them what time we have, starting now."

Harper's shoulder drooped and she let out an acquiescent groan. "All right, all right. Guilt trip successful."

Lily crossed her arms and gave me a disappointed look. "And I suppose I have no choice in the matter, considering?"

"Correct."

"What about my ankle?"

"You're literally at Angie's bakery now and the law hasn't descended upon you, have they?"

Greta leaned to the side to peek through the front display window. "Suppose not."

I felt a pair of arms wrap around my waist as Angie squeezed me tight. "Thank you so much, you guys. This is a life saver."

Shelby wiped a tear from the corner of her eye. "With so many hands, we'll make light work of it, dearies. Just make sure to keep Mason away from me or else I'll wring his pimply little neck."

I clapped my hands together. "Okay, where do we start? I have a date with Ryan later, and I'd hate to cancel."

Shelby popped up from her chair. "Let's head to the diner, dearies. We'll raid the larder and see what we can put together. With the time we have left, we'll be lucky to make a fraction of what we need."

"Don't worry," I said to Angie and Shelby, "I'm sure the food and everything will go smoothly tomorrow. No bumps, no issues. Just smooth sailing."

***

Shelby guarded the kitchen's back door like a beehived hawk, and unless a fire broke out, no soul would pass through without facing her wrath. The four of us, along with Mason, scurried from station to station recreating the appetizers under Shelby's pointed direction.

Mason winced at every scathing reprimand that flew from Shelby's mouth. While I felt a bit sorry for the teenager, the fact was, we were sweating our tushies off because of Mason's negligence. He was wise to keep his head down and hands busy.

After an hour, I needed a break from the food prepping, so I slipped out the front door of the diner, careful to avoid Shelby. I slung my apron over my shoulder and breathed the sea air deeply. I had no idea how stifling commercial kitchens could be. I missed my own light and airy kitchen at the Pearl, even the broken smart toaster.

Pastor Basil, Lovie, and Benjamin Locke gathered in front of the bookstore. I remembered that the bookstore owner had stopped by the Pearl looking for me, and a tickle of curiosity ran through me. *Was he announcing his opening?* But it was clear from my perspective across the street that the windows were still covered over.

I checked that Shelby wasn't looking before jogging over to join the three on the sidewalk. Pastor Basil and Benjamin greeted me with wide, friendly smiles.

"Good afternoon, Poppy," Pastor Basil said. "We were just asking Mr. Locke when the bookstore might open."

At the mention of Benjamin, I couldn't help but size him up. Tailored khaki pants and a fitted long-sleeve shirt skirted the muscles of his arms and shoulders. "I heard you came by the Pearl. Was there something you needed?"

He smiled broadly. "Not at all. In fact, I came by to bring you this." He dug a hand into a leather satchel at his side and pulled out a book.

"What's this?" I asked, taking the book from his outstretched hand.

"Something I thought you might enjoy."

I ran a hand over the beautiful, embossed cover. Pastor Basil and Lovie waited eagerly to know what gift the new resident had given me, eyeing me curiously. I read the title aloud for their benefit. "Victorian Architecture of the Pacific Northwest 1800-1900."

"Your house is so *iconic*," Benjamin said. "A perfect specimen of the era. It's featured on page seventy-two." He pointed to a ribbon sticking from between the pages. "I've marked it there."

"Thank you," I said with honest gratitude. "That's so thoughtful." I opened the book gingerly to the marked page and set the ribbon aside. The book's pages had that enchanting patina and smell that only come with age. An ink drawing filled the left side page. I recognized the Pearl immediately. I'd seen that exact perspective every time I turned onto the roundabout and the Pearl came into view. To the right was a photograph from a similar angle, all in gray tones that didn't do the vibrant purple paint justice. Still beautiful, still stately, and hardly changed at all since it had passed to me from my uncle, Arthur, which had been passed down to him all the way from our ancestor, Claude Goodwin. Even the renovations I'd made where hidden from public view to preserve the integrity and history of the house.

"What a lovely gift," Lovie said. Her eyes flitted from Benjamin to me and back again. "A very *personalized* gift."

"Is that book from your shelves inside?" Pastor Basil motioned to the sealed-up bookstore behind us. "Don't keep us waiting, man. When are you opening?"

Benjamin held up his hands. "I know you're eager, but it's not quite ready for the masses."

"I hear plenty of noise coming from inside. At all hours, too." Lovie's voice was disapproving. "Not sure what you're remodeling, but it must be impressive."

Benjamin dropped his eyes shyly. "It's a lot of work, I'll say that much."

"I'm not sure why all the secrecy," I said, "but I'm sure it will be worth it in the end."

"Thank you," he said. "Now, why are you dressed up that way?"

I looked down at my clothes, having forgotten about my catering uniform and the apron over my shoulder. "Little mishap, so we're doing some last-minute preparations for the upcoming wedding. I should get back to the diner soon."

"Ah, hello there," came a Scottish accent from behind me.

Ryan appeared, clad in a simple pant and green V-neck sweater, and held out his hand to the new bookstore owner. "Ryan MacKenzie. Nice to meet you…"

"Benjamin Locke."

"Welcome to Starry Cove." Ryan's voice was suddenly two-pitches more baritone.

I side-eyed him. "What happened to your voice?"

Ryan coughed. "Nothing. What's that?" He pointed to the book in my hand.

I ran a hand delicately over the embossing on the cover. "It's a book about my house. Benjamin thought I'd appreciate it."

"Did he?" Ryan's voice broke, and he coughed to clear it out. "How nice." He smiled, but it didn't reach his eyes.

Benjamin didn't seem to notice. "I saw it and thought of you immediately."

Ryan's arm casually wrapped around my shoulder. "Ready for tonight?"

"About that…"

Ryan's face fell, but one half-glance at Benjamin and he caught himself.

"I need to help Angie and Shelby, but I think we'll be done in time. Pick me up at six?"

He beamed, puffing out the V-neck of his sweater.

"I'd better get back to the diner. Shelby's probably looking for me." I stepped off the sidewalk toward the diner, but turned around. "And Ryan, you should probably keep a closer eye on Daisy."

Thirteen

COVERED IN FLOUR, grease, and caramelized onions, I finally tore myself away from Shelby's Diner and headed back to the Pearl to get ready for my date with Ryan. We'd made good progress on the appetizers, and I felt good taking off. Even Shelby hadn't held me back. Surprisingly, Greta chose to stay. I think the opportunity to work in a commercial kitchen proved too good a temptation.

I rounded a hedge along the sidewalk that stretched along the roundabout. I spied Jennifer on the lawn, near the butt pile, and narrowed my eyes. Caught in the act! I scurried up the walk. She spotted me and quickly stubbed out her cigarette and made for the door.

"Hey," I shouted. "Don't run away from me."

I caught her just as she reached for the doorknob. A look of guilt draped over her face.

"Were you smoking just there?" I sniffed the general air surrounding her.

"I don't know what you're talking about."

"Don't play innocent," I said.

She shook her head vigorously. "Not me."

"I found a pile of cigarette butts earlier. Are they yours? I saw you toss one just now into the same place."

Her eyes turned downcast. "Oh dear."

"So, it *was* you. And what about this?" I pulled out the crumpled note I'd found along with the butts.

Her face drained of color.

"Care to explain this note? It's clearly from Charmaine to you. Apparently, you hadn't just met the other day."

Jennifer fell into the nearest bench along the covered porch. She put a hand to her stomach as if ill.

"Are you all right?" I asked.

She waved me off. "I just need a moment."

I placed myself between Jennifer and any escape from the porch, not really concerned that she'd make a break for it, but to lessen enticement nonetheless.

Finally, she spoke. "You're right that I knew Charmaine before a few days ago. I almost died from shock when she walked in, and I know she was surprised, too. I could see it on her face. She was always one to let you know how she felt."

"How long did you know her? This note seems awfully personal."

Jennifer shied away, averting her eyes. "We met at college. We were roommates in the first-year dorms. I'd never been away from my family in the suburbs and she seemed so worldly. I assumed she grew up in a big city since she was so vivacious and confident. Imagine my surprise when she told me she grew up on an actual commune. It seems so long ago." Jennifer shook her head as if to free herself of the memory. "It wasn't long after the beginning of that freshman year that I started breaking out of my shell. I think without my family, I was able to really experiment, you know?"

"That's what college is for."

She let out a blip of a laugh. "Needless to say, Charmaine was a big part of my life then. Parties, smoking and drinking, boys and..."

"And what?"

Jennifer straightened her back and took a deep breath. "And girls. Charmaine was my first. We had a bit of a love affair you might call it. Being roommates helped. It was only a phase, though. I was breaking so many rules it was just another swat at my conservative upbringing. You've met my mother and Chad. I've crawled back into my shell, now." She let out a wistful sigh. "Those college days were the best time of my life. But it couldn't last. And if my family found out..."

"They'd ostracize you?"

She nodded. "I never kicked the smoking habit, though. That one's been hard to hide. I've been sneaking in and out. I'm sorry about hiding them in your bushes."

"What about Charmaine's note?"

Jennifer's face hardened at mention of the note. "That first night, I tried to avoid her. I knew that with my family in town, the truth could come out too easily, so I thought it best to pretend we'd never met. Charmaine played along at first, but I think when she realized I wasn't going to drop the act, it wasn't fun anymore. She handed me that note in passing."

"Ziggy said she saw you two talking that first night. Was that when she handed you the note?"

Jennifer nodded again. "Yes, it must be. That was the only real interaction we had. I seized up at the thought of her telling my family about us."

I shifted my feet, wary of what that fear may have led to. "You were scared of her?"

"I was scared of what she could do, but not her. Those are very different things."

"Sounds like you had a reason to stop her."

"I know what you're thinking," Jennifer said, "but you're wrong. I had nothing to do with Charmaine's murder. There are plenty of other women here who have a lifetime of hatred and animosity."

"She could have ruined your life. That sounds like enough."

"I couldn't have done it. I was out here on the porch all night, chain-smoking out of breathless anxiety at what she might say or do in front of my family."

"You were out here?"

"That's right. Just here, on the porch."

I thought back to that first night. All the door alarms. The pile of cigarette butts I'd attributed to the Smarty Pants technician—they had been Jennifer's all along. But she couldn't have been responsible for all the door alarms. I tried to remember how many times the alarm sounded Three? Four? I couldn't recall how often I'd slapped my phone to turn it off.

"You believe me, right?" Jennifer's voice was unsteady.

"Did anyone see you?" I asked. "Did you see anyone else?"

Jennifer wilted. "No one else. I suppose that doesn't look too good."

"It doesn't look great." Without memory of the number of times the alarm went off, I couldn't quite piece together Saffron's walkabout and Jennifer's chain-smoking escapade. Both would have set the alarm off twice, once leaving, and once returning. That's four. And if Jennifer didn't see anyone, and Saffron was the last to arrive, then Jennifer must have come back inside before Saffron returned. My head was already spinning. "I need to wrap my head around all this."

Jennifer slumped into the bench, looking sad and a bit fearful.

"I won't tell anyone about you and Charmaine. For now," I added when she perked up. "Just don't give me another reason to even suspect you had a part in this."

Jennifer nodded, her brown hair flopping over her shoulders. "Of course. I appreciate your discretion. And I assure you, I had nothing to do with Charmaine's murder. I was just as shocked as the others."

"Yeah," I said, "but one of those *shocked* others is the one who did it. Assurances don't hold much weight when a murderer is afoot."

"I want this solved as much as you do," Jennifer said. "If I can help in any way, let me know. And no more cigarette butts, I promise."

"Keep your eyes and ears open. If you hear anything—and I mean anything—let me know right away." I'd grown so tired over the course of the day that I'd dropped my guard with Jennifer, but if the culprit were to out themselves, I'd need everyone on alert.

***

I left Jennifer on the porch to continue her chain smoking

and entered the house. Recognizing her short blonde hair, Heavenleigh was alone in the common room, perusing a shelf of books and collectibles, some left over from my late uncle. I eased my hand into one pocket and fingered the set of Charmaine's earrings I had stowed in my pocket earlier. As I approached, Heavenleigh ran her hand over a particularly interesting artifact—a small copper figurine of a ship. "Pretty neat, huh?" I asked her.

She jumped at my voice. "Oh, yes. You startled me."

"That's a replica of the Queen Anne's Revenge, Blackbeard's pirate ship."

"How fascinating. All your things are."

"Funny," I said, stepping closer to Heavenleigh's side. "Some of my fascinating things have gone missing recently."

"Oh?" She ran a finger along one sail of the figurine.

"Yes. And I had a chance to catch up with my friend, Charlie. She owns the store you and the other's visited the other day."

"Oh?"

"If I recall, you showed me something you bought there."

Heavenleigh tapped her lip. "Did I?"

I stepped closer and dug a hand into my pocket and pulled out the jewelry I'd found tucked under the dresser in Heavenleigh's room. "Care to tell me why these were in your room?"

The young woman looked down at the jewelry in my palm and shook her head. "I don't know why those were in my room. I've never seen them before. Have you asked Maya? Although, they don't look like something she'd wear."

"These were hidden under a dresser. Stowed away like black market contraband."

She shrugged. "I don't know what to tell you."

"How about if I told you these were Charmaine's, what then? They were missing from her body the night she was murdered."

Heavenleigh looked as confused as before.

"I know you lied about buying something from Charlie's store."

She stiffened. "I did not. How dare you—"

"What were you doing when Charmaine was killed?"

Heavenleigh took a step back, bracing herself against the back of the nearby sofa. "I was in my room. I had to use the bathroom at some point, I guess. Yes, that's right. I left to use the restroom. I wasn't feeling well. Maya can vouch for me."

My face grew hot knowing Heavenleigh was lying to me. Ziggy, drunk as a skunk, had occupied the upstairs bathroom most of the night, that I was sure of. "You're lying. I know it."

"I most surely am not. Ask Maya. I left to use the restroom and came back a little while later."

"Impossible. Ziggy was in that bathroom all night."

I could practically see the gears turning in her head.

"Maybe Charmaine knew what you were up to," I said. "Someone told me they saw you two having a heated conversation. Perhaps you stole something from her?" I gave the jewelry in my hand a little shake.

"I'd never take from Charmaine," Heavenleigh said. "She'd have caught me." As soon as the words were out, she clapped a hand over her mouth.

"But you'd steal from others?" I pressed harder,

closing in on her.

She gulped, averting her eyes anywhere but at mine. She tried to find a way out, but I'd blocked her in. Finally, her shoulders gave out. "Okay, you've found me out. I may have taken a few items from your friend's shop, but nothing big." She stared at her toes. "Never big."

"Never big?"

Her voice had grown meek. "I never take anything big, only small, lovely things. They draw me in and I can't help myself. A pen here, a dainty book there. They find their way into my bag and I can't stop them."

"So, you're a thief. The things that have gone missing around here were you, too."

She nodded slowly. "When I left my room that night, I didn't go to the bathroom. I came downstairs to look at all the lovely things I'd seen that night. I wanted to touch them all, just touch them." Her face was earnest, wide-eyed and innocent. "Then, somehow, they wind up in my pockets."

I made a mental inventory of all my missing items, cursing myself since I'd now owe Greta an apology, something I was loath to do. "Back to Charmaine. Why should I believe you? You've been caught in a bunch of lies just now."

"Honestly, Poppy. I know it's a lot to ask you to believe me, but I never went into Charmaine's room and I never took her jewelry. When I passed by, I heard voices coming from inside and I kept right on down the stairs."

"Voices? Whose?"

She gave a little shrug. "I assumed it was Charmaine and Saffron."

I pursed my lips. *Not Saffron, but who?* "I still can't

trust that you aren't lying."

"I was only downstairs for a little while. Ask Maya."

"I'll do that, and I suggest you return those items before I tell Charlie what I know. I don't appreciate people stealing from my friends." I pointed a stern finger at her. "And I expect *all* my missing items to find their way back by the time I return tonight."

Heavenleigh heaved a sigh of relief and nodded earnestly. "Of course. Absolutely."

I tucked the jewelry into my pocket. "Glad that's settled. Now, excuse me, I need to get ready for a date with my boyfriend."

***

Ryan and I made our way to Vista, humorously selecting the restaurant where we had our first real date, Troppa Pasta, and where Ryan had boldly selected the special which turned out to be tentacles in white sauce.

We cruised down a familiar road past an even more familiar strip mall. "Hey, that's Madam Mystica's Divination Den where we went yesterday."

"Divination?" The word sounded strange with Ryan's Scottish accent.

"Long story," I said.

"What did you find out? Is there adventure in your future? Maybe a lottery jackpot."

"She said to be wary of Scotsmen."

Ryan grumbled behind the wheel and I gave him a playful nudge.

"It's all poppycock anyway," he said as the strip mall faded into the distance behind us.

A few minutes later and we were seated at our table.

I let out a sigh as I sat down.

"What's wrong?" he asked.

"It's this wedding tomorrow. We ran in circles today to make up for your dog's diner disaster with Dewey."

Ryan smirked. "Daisy's a wandering soul."

"Well, she could wander less close to Shelby's kitchen door. How can a dog that small eat that many appetizers?"

"You said Dewey helped."

"Bottomless pits, both of them. Oh good." The waiter arrived with our bread sticks. We put in our orders, then I grabbed two sticks and started munching on the first.

"You've got an appetite today."

I waited until I could form words through the chewing. "I've been run ragged by Shelby all afternoon, not to mention the drama with the wedding. Part ravenous hunger and part stress-eating."

"The wedding will be over tomorrow, so that should alleviate some of it, eh?"

I sighed into a bite of bread. "It's also Lily. Greta, too."

"I hope you and Lily aren't fighting again."

Without trying to bore him, I shared Lily's financial predicament. "I just want her to be independent. And I'm sick of sharing a bed with Greta. I'd sleep on the sofa if I didn't care what my guests thought." A shiver ran down my back at the thought of Greta's toenails dragging down my leg again.

"Can't say the idea of spending a night with Greta appeals much to me, either."

"I hope I haven't ruined your appetite," I said. "Greta does that a lot."

He chuckled. "Tell me about this wedding. You said I get to wear my kilt, so I'm quite chuffed."

"The wedding," I said with a groan. "Don't remind me about tomorrow. I'm worried about Saffron—that's the bride. Her nerves are all frazzled. She fainted at the rehearsal. Did you hear about that?"

He shook his head.

"The bridesmaid who's a doctor has been caring for her, I guess. Poor doctor has been playing nurse to all these tragic women."

"She can prescribe something for nerves or anxiety," Ryan said.

I twirled the second bread stick. "She seems reluctant. I can't blame her, either. One of the ladies is a total drunk and most of them seem a little off kilter in one way or another. I can't say I won't be relieved when the wedding is finally over and the Pearl is quiet again."

"Aye, but you'll still have Greta." He followed this with a wink.

Our waiter returned with our food, and without hesitation, I dug into my linguine. I let the carbs wrap me in a warm hug before allowing my mind to settle back on Greta. "She's completely sabotaged my new smart home. I'm finding toothpicks shoved into every nook and cranny. The toaster is complete toast."

Ryan shoveled a forkful of spaghetti into his mouth and let me drone on. I got the impression he was trying to avoid eye contact.

"What is it?" I asked. "Why aren't you saying anything?"

He dabbed at the corners of his mouth with his napkin and cleared his throat. "It seems like this smart home

Lucinda Harrison

isn't all sunshine and flowers. Maybe it's causing more problems that it's worth."

"Greta is the problem."

He shifted slightly in his chair. "Didn't you mention trouble with your door alarm?"

"Greta sabotaged it."

"No," he said. "Earlier than that. The first night."

I nodded. "The night Charmaine was murdered. It kept going off and waking me up. It was just Dewey setting off the—"

Ryan looked up from his food at my sudden stop. "What is it?"

"The technician said there was nothing wrong with my sensor."

Ryan cocked his head. "I don't follow what you mean."

I stared toward the far wall in the restaurant, focusing on nothing but reliving the alarms in my mind. *Nothing wrong with the sensor.* One, two, three, four, five, and six. I jolted back to stare intensely at Ryan. "The alarm went off *six* times."

"Okay." He drew the word out as if expecting me to elaborate.

"Six times, not four. Jennifer and Jennifer. Saffron and Saffron. Who else?"

Ryan shook his head. "Still lost."

"The alarm went off six times the night Charmaine died. It wasn't a faulty sensor picking up Dewey. Four of those alarms were one of my guests—Jennifer—leaving and returning. She's a chain-smoker." I added the last bit when Ryan still seemed confused. "Two other times were Saffron, the bride, heading out to perform her secret ritual then returning."

He sputtered, choking on a noodle. "Her what?"

I ignored him and continued. "But that means someone else left the house. Two more alarms. Someone else leaving and returning." I tapped my fork on my plate. "But who?"

"Sorry," Ryan said, "I think I misheard you. Did you say *secret ritual*?"

"If I assume Jennifer was telling me the truth and remove her and Saffron from the equation, that only leaves four able-bodied women in the house with Charmaine: Clover, Kismet, Maya, and Heavenleigh. Heavenleigh said she heard voices coming from Charmaine's room but that she was downstairs for only a little while, and Maya could vouch for that. How long does it take to murder someone?"

Chatter and the clanking of utensils from nearby tables stopped abruptly. Various sets of eyes turned my way. I froze, mortified that I'd let myself blabber on so loudly. Eventually, the restaurant patrons returned to their dinners, and I gave Ryan an apologetic smile.

"You sure know how to turn heads," he said.

I rolled my eyes and returned to my pasta.

"You caught that new bookstore owner's eye today."

"I was just being friendly."

"He's already plying you with gifts."

"You act like he gave me flowers or chocolates or something. It was a book about old-timey houses. Very romantic." I let the sarcasm drip, but a little pang inside had to admit the gift had felt special. Personal even, as Lovie had said. Not that I was going to admit anything to Ryan. It was all just silly fun, anyway.

"Aye," he said. "That's how it starts. Take it from a man who's wooed once or twice before. I know what's on his mind."

"This jealous side of you is kind of charming. You puff up like a little Scottish bulldog."

He frowned.

I reached across the table and lay my hand on his. "Don't fret, little bulldog. I'm still yours."

His frown turned into a smile.

"As long as you wear your kilt to the wedding," I added, returning his smile. "Otherwise, the deal's off."

***

Dinner fun was over and Ryan dropped me back at the Pearl around ten that evening. I'd spotted Kismet on the porch from the passenger seat of Ryan's car. She was alone, seated on one of the benches, her face illuminated from the glow of her cell phone. An enormous grin shone on her face. *Time to find out who this Gardener fellow really is.*

As I exited the car, her phone clicked off and along with it, the blue light from the screen. I approached the porch and stepped up the few stairs leading to the door. Kismet remained silent and motionless. I suspected she thought I might miss her since the bench was bathed in near darkness. "Good evening," I said.

"Oh, hello Poppy." Kismet's manufactured surprised was obvious. "Where have you been?"

"I was out for dinner. It's a bit chilly to be sitting out here in the dark, isn't it?"

"Is it? I hadn't noticed. I guess I've gotten used to how cold it is by the ocean after a week."

"Mm-hmm. And how is Gardener doing?" I let the name linger a bit as I said it, drawing it out for emphasis.

Her dark silhouette froze. "What do you mean?"

"Gardener," I repeated. "The man you've been texting."

She sat forward, closer to the light so her features could be seen. She was not happy. "How do you know about him?"

"You don't hide it very well," I said. "You're practically glued to your phone with a silly schoolgirl grin on your face."

"It's not what you think."

"It's exactly what I think."

Kismet's face set. "All right. It is. So what?"

"So, you—" But I hadn't really thought about why it mattered, only that Kismet was being dishonest. My only take on Kismet's motive to kill Charmaine was jealousy over her husband and a desire to become the Maid of Honor, which seemed a flimsy motive now. With her own lover, 'so, what?' was the right question. I settled on the only string I had left to pull. "So you've been dishonest."

Her head flew back and she let out a cackle. "Dishonest? Welcome to the club, lady." She crossed her arms and leaned against the house.

"This doesn't seem like a good time to be dishonest with anyone. Charmaine is dead, remember?"

"Oh, I remember," she said with a hint of a smile. "How could I forget?"

"Aren't you scared that her affair with your husband will come out? That you have the strongest, most compelling motive to murder Charmaine? The scorned wife."

"I don't care if everyone finds out. My marriage is

over, I've found someone else." The confidence in her voice was almost mocking. "And most important of all, I didn't kill Charmaine."

"Prove it." I tried to make my tone as commanding as Kismet's. "You were the only one who knew Charmaine would be alone in her room."

"Can you be sure of that? Besides, I was out here the whole time." She pointed to my yard, toward a small bench that sat among the foliage. "Exchanging messages with Gardener." She held out her phone to me. "Here, see for yourself."

I shied away from the light so Kismet couldn't see me blushing. I'd read a few of those messages. "How do I know you were out here when you sent those? Did anyone see you?"

"No," she admitted, "but I saw someone else."

"Who?"

"I'm not sure. I saw a glowing light in the dark, though, over and over. Someone smoking, I think. I didn't want to be seen, so I was stuck out here until whoever it was decided to go back inside."

The lump in my throat seemed to grow. Their stories added up. Kismet *was* out here that night, and she saw Jennifer smoking. Kismet leaving and returning—those were the two missing door alarms.

"You look like you swallowed a toad. Are you okay?"

"Yes," I said, swallowing the toad with a gulp. "Did this person do anything else?"

Kismet shrugged. "No. Just sat where I am now and lit one after another."

I decided to prod her a bit longer. "If you left your

room, that means Jennifer was left alone. She could have killed Charmaine."

Kismet scrunched her face. "That doesn't make any sense. Why would she? They'd just met. Sure, Charmaine was a stuck-up monster, but I doubt even she could turn someone against her that fast." She tapped her chin mockingly. "Actually, she probably could."

I disliked Kismet's flippancy, but couldn't refute what she claimed.

"Are you done interrogating me?" she asked. "It's getting cold out here."

I stepped aside and let her enter the warmth of the Pearl while I remained outside. The cold air hit me too, but I wanted it to keep me sharp. Both stories matched up. The piles of cigarettes, the salacious text messages. Kismet even accounted for the remaining door alarms. It all fit, and now I knew exactly who was in the house that night. Three little bridesmaids all in a row, and I had very important questions for each of them.

The Pearl was quiet as I stepped through the entryway. I half expected to find Heavenleigh skulking about and fondling all my trinkets, but after checking around, the missing items I'd blamed on Greta had found their way back to their rightful spots. I grimaced at the thought of apologizing to my housekeeper, but I had to own up to my misplaced assumptions. I'd save that chore for tomorrow. Big wedding aside, it was going to be an interesting day.

Fourteen

MULTIPLE SCRIPTS RAN through my head as Greta and I worked in the kitchen early the following morning. *It has come to my attention that you were not guilty of the crime of...* I shook my head. That wouldn't work at all. *Remember when I accused you of stealing? Oops, my bad. Ugh!* I glanced at Greta stirring an enormous pot at the stove, hips swaying atop her stool to a tune only she could hear. Gritting my teeth, I called her name, "Greta?"

She grunted an acknowledgement.

"I need to tell you something."

Another grunt.

"I'm sorry."

She grunted a third time, but continued stirring.

Phew. I quickly turned back to my own task. That had been easier than I thought, but then I wondered if her quick dismissal meant she'd misunderstood. I frowned at her tiny back, but chose to let it go. I'd take a misunderstood dismissal over dragging out a long, difficult apology.

The swivel door swung open and Clover walked through with a cheeriness in her step. "Good morning," she said. "Just need to check on my kombucha." She made her way to the fridge, where her bottles had commandeered a good portion of the space. "I'm hoping some of the wedding guests are looking to invest, so I want to bring a good selection. Maybe the Kokonut?"

I tossed my dishtowel onto the counter. "I've been meaning to ask you something, Clover."

She popped up from the fridge, eyes bright. "You finally want to invest in Klover Kombucha?"

"Um, no. At the rehearsal dinner, Ziggy mentioned that you weren't in your room the night Charmaine died. At least, not the whole night."

Clover cocked her head as if thinking. "I don't really remember."

"She said you weren't there when she left for the bathroom."

Clover rolled her eyes. "Her trip to the bathroom. Poor girl. She was so drunk, I doubt she could remember much of anything. You probably shouldn't worry about it."

"And someone else said they heard voices coming from Charmaine's room. Two people talking."

Clover's eyes shifted to anywhere but me. "Really? Probably Char and Saffy."

I gave a slow, considering nod, then said, "It wasn't Saffron."

Any slight movement ceased as Clover froze like a deer in headlights.

"Was it you in that room with Charmaine?"

She didn't answer.

"There was one of your kombucha bottles next to Charmaine's body. I haven't forgotten that. Perhaps all this pushing for financial replacements meant you knew Charmaine would be out of the picture."

Clover looked to the fridge, toward her cache of kombucha. "I didn't kill her."

"So, it *was* you in the room?"

She nodded. "I was so frustrated at her. I'd had enough of her interpretation of *silent partner*. That first night, when she told me to put hard kombucha on the board agenda, I about blew up then and there. No financial backing is worth dealing with Charmaine. It was like a deal with the devil, but it was the only way I could get off the ground."

"You aren't really convincing me you had nothing to do with her murder. All this sounds like a perfect motive."

"Right." She cleared her throat. "I planned to talk to Charmaine that night. Ziggy had passed out, so I decided that was as good a time as any to finally break it off with her. I'd been mulling what I was going to say all night. Reasons, excuses, that sort of thing. But really, I just hated working with her. I knocked first, and Charmaine let me in. Saffron wasn't there, at least. That would have made it more awkward."

"How so?"

"I was basically breaking up with her, business-wise. You don't want all that out in the open."

"You admit you were in there alone with her?"

"Yes, but I didn't attack her or anything. I told her I wanted her out of my business. We were done. Klover Kombucha was moving on."

"And how did Charmaine respond to that? I find it

hard to believe she just rolled over. She didn't fight it?"

"No." When Clover saw my disbelief, she continued, "I was surprised, too. But that nasty—" She caught herself and ran a hand across the Klover Kombucha branding on her shirt, taking a moment to regain some composure. "But she said she was fine with it. Said she wanted off the 'sinking ship' as she called it."

My eyes narrowed. "You're getting angry just recalling it."

"Of course I'm angry," she spat. "She ran my business into the ground with all of her suggestions and demands, threatening to pull her backing if I didn't do what she wanted, and she had the gall to call it a *sinking ship*. Ha!"

Clover's cackle even started Greta, who wobbled on her stool. I was thankful she continued cooking and didn't interfere with our conversation, although I was sure she was listening to every word.

"Anyway," Clover said, jutting out her chin, "that's why I've been looking for another investor—to buy out Charmaine. She would have been gone either way, even without dying, although that spiked my urgency."

"What about the kombucha bottle?"

Her hand flung to the side toward the fridge. "She was always drinking a Klover Kombucha. She couldn't keep herself away from the stuff. It's *delicious*. I left her with it. After her 'sinking ship' comment, I was done. I went back to my room and left her there, very much alive, thank you very much."

"Did you see anyone else?"

She shook her head. "I'd fallen asleep, but Ziggy came back eventually since she was in our room when we were woken up by Saffron screaming. And that's it. I left the room once to confront Charmaine. I have nothing to hide. Now, if you'll excuse me, I need to get ready for the wedding." Clover brushed by me and disappeared through the swivel door.

"Nice lady," Greta said, still stirring.

I waited for the door to stop swinging. "Her story tracks, but she's got no one to confirm any of it, only Charmaine."

Greta chuckled. "And Charmaine sure isn't talking."

I frowned at her poor taste. "Are you almost done? We need to change into our uniforms and get to the church soon. And I still need to wrangle Lily, as well."

She hopped off the stool and landed with a thud, then rubbed her hands together. "Yep, I'm ready to go."

With the wedding mere hours away, it dawned on me that I was running out of time to figure out which of these bridesmaids had turned on Charmaine. I'd be preoccupied at the wedding reception, but I still hadn't narrowed it down enough. There were important pieces still missing.

***

I dragged Greta and Lily behind me, Lily protesting the entire way to the church.

"I don't see why we have to wear these ghastly uniforms to the ceremony. Isn't there a place to change?"

"There won't be time," I said. "The reception is right after and we're expected to be ready. At least you get to wear your hat."

My sister lifted a hand to her hat, which sat daintily atop her head and skewed at just the right angle to be fashionable. A single peacock feather decorated one side, and it flounced with each step we took. "Why are we attending this wedding, anyway? You don't even know these people."

I stopped in the middle of the sidewalk and they both screeched to a halt behind me. I rounded on Lily. "Saffron was kind enough to invite us to her wedding. This is an important day for her. Would you rather sit and mope or dare to let a little happiness seep into your life?"

Lily flinched.

"I don't know about you," Greta said, "but I love weddings. All the romance and family tiffs really hit the spot."

I took this moment on the sidewalk to give our group a once-over. Greta's uniform was oversized, with six inches of rolled cuff to account for her short stature. She was a lost cause. Lily's uniform, however, had been impeccably cleaned and ironed—no doubt by Greta—and her chic designer hat, complete with flouncing peacock feather, contrasted with the simple one I wore which was more practical than anything. It was my sad attempt to glam up for the wedding, but next to Lily's effortless fashion, I felt more than a bit frumpy.

We reached the church after a few minutes' walk, joining the other guests who milled around the area before the ceremony was scheduled to begin. We made our way inside, and I immediately sought out Angie. After yesterday's prep work, she'd surely have instructions for us regarding the reception. I spotted Harper first, tall and lanky. Her dark brown curls tied up with a rainbow ribbon. She towered over the sea of beige that made up the groom's extended family.

I weaved us through the crowd toward Harper. Angie

wouldn't be far away. After clearing the mass of beige, we finally reached them. "How's everything going?" I asked Angie.

Angie's face was sheer anxiety. "Everything should be ready, although you know with these things something is bound to go wrong."

"She's been like this all morning," Harper said. "Doom and gloom."

"But we got everything prepped yesterday. That should have gotten the food to where it needed to be for today."

Angie nodded. "I know, but my stomach is still churning. Greta was a great help though." Angie leaned past me and gave Greta a big smile.

Lily stared down at the tiny old woman and scowled. I held back a grin. My sister was not used to being subpar at anything, and she definitely didn't like someone as uncouth as Greta getting all the accolades.

"Shelby and I still burned the midnight oil last night, so I'm pretty pooped today. You know I'm not used to staying up late."

Harper scoffed. "Your version of midnight oil is probably about eight in the evening."

Angie bristled. "It was eleven. Late, anyway. The whole town was quiet when we left the diner except for the bookstore. Mr. Locke must be working really hard to open that shop. Lots of banging and knocking going on."

At mention of Benjamin Locke, I tried to suppress my grin.

"Why are you grinning like a schoolgirl?" Harper asked.

"It's nothing," I said. "Benjamin gifted me a lovely

book yesterday about old houses. The Pearl was featured inside."

Angie and Harper both raised eyebrows at me.

"What?"

"And how does Ryan feel about this gift?" Angie asked.

"It was just a friendly gesture."

"Your grin doesn't say friendly to me." Harper said.

Angie nodded, "More like come-hither. Isn't Ryan your date today?"

"Yes, and he's wearing a kilt just for me." I tried to make my voice reassert Ryan as my beau-of-choice.

"Look," Angie said, pointing through a door off the nave. "The bridesmaids are arriving. I'm sure they'll be getting ready in the back rooms. We should find our seats."

The bridesmaids filed in one-by-one, dressed in long, flowy seafoam, and disappeared down a side hallway. From afar, I thought Saffron had dressed the same as the bridesmaids, but then I quickly realized it was Heavenleigh with her hair pinned up. It was easy to mix the two up if you weren't looking closely.

I turned to my friends. "If you sit by Ryan, I'll find you guys in a minute. I want to go talk to the ladies."

I slipped through the door into a hallway that led to Pastor Basil's office and a few extra rooms used for storage, now co-opted to serve as preparation rooms for the wedding party. The bridesmaids had disappeared into one set of these rooms by the time I came by, although I wasn't sure which one.

"Poppy, thank heavens," a voice called from behind me.

I spun around to see Saffron, decked in full gauzy, flowy, wedding regalia. Like the bridesmaids' dresses, it was airy and light, but instead of seafoam, the dress was various tones of ivory with decorative embroidery cascading down the sleeves and the short train that trailed behind her.

"I need your help."

"What is it?" I asked, suddenly worried something had gone terribly wrong at the eleventh hour.

"I snagged a button, and it's come loose on my dress. I can't find Kismet or the others. Can you help?"

A wave of relief passed over me. "Sure. Shouldn't be too hard."

Saffron spun around and I found the errant button. A few loose threads dangled from it, and with a tug or two, it tightened right up. "There you go."

"Oh, thank you so much. I'd normally ask Kizzy, but I don't want to run around and snag anything else."

I glanced down the hall, but it was all quiet, just the distant buzz of the filling church. Saffron and I were alone. "I've been meaning to ask you something. You never gave me a straight answer about why Charmaine was your Maid of Honor. It seems so much like Kismet would have been your first choice."

Saffron's face took on a worried look. She bit one side of her bottom lip and skirted her eyes. "It's complicated, Poppy, and I'm sure it wouldn't interest you."

"Actually," I said, doing my best to fill the hallway space, "it interests me quite a lot."

Saffron peered over my shoulder as if checking for other people, then her face turned downcast. "Promise you won't say anything?"

"That depends on what you share. Is it something illegal?"

"What?" she sputtered. "No, no." She shook her head, and the crystals decorating her curls jingled. "It's about Heavenleigh."

"Heavenleigh?" There was surprise in my voice, but Heavenleigh was still on my short list. I waited for the ball to drop. What did Saffron know?

"I'm sure you've heard that the commune was very close-knit. Everyone was friendly. It was a very *loving* community."

This was not going in the direction I'd expected. The confusion must have shown on my face because Saffron didn't continue.

"Should I go on?" she asked.

My trepidation had waned, but I nodded for her to continue.

"So, in this very loving community, people grow close. Very close. It's a natural thing and there is no shame in it. It's healthy, if you think of it that way."

"What are you getting at?"

She huffed and tossed her arms up, clearly frustrated. "What I'm trying to say is, Heavenleigh is my sister."

I gaped. "Your sister?"

"Shh! Lower your voice." Saffron checked the hallway behind us for any eavesdroppers.

I'd have been less surprised if Saffron blurted out that Heavenleigh was an alien. "Does she know? How long has this… Who…"

Saffron's shoulders wilted. "She doesn't know. At least, I don't think she does. I only found out a few months ago that Papa Zamora is my father. My daddy—

the one I thought was my dad—is out in the crowd right now. He can't find out. It would destroy him. I'm his little baby girl."

My mouth started and stopped a number of times, each time no words formed. Finally, I asked her, "How did you find out?"

"That's what I was getting at," she said. "It was Charmaine, of course. I don't know how she found out, but it's true. Look at Heavenleigh and look at me. It's hard to tell the two of us apart. I'm surprised we never caught on."

I thought of Lily and our own similarities. Others saw it, but only when forced to look did either of us acknowledge that there was any resemblance. As a stranger, I'd mistaken Saffron for Heavenleigh and vice versa, yet I'd never put it together until now, either. "I think I know what you mean."

"And Charmaine being Charmaine, decided it was too good a nugget not to exploit. She demanded to be my Maid of Honor, otherwise she'd spill the secret to everyone, even my daddy. I couldn't let that happen."

"So, that's why you chose Charmaine over Kismet?"

Saffron nodded slowly. "I knew it would break Kizzy's heart, but I couldn't tell her why. I had to come up with some pathetic story about being torn between two friends, when really, I was being blackmailed." She jerked up straight. "Yes, that's it—I was being blackmailed by Charmaine. I've never put those words to it, but that's exactly what was happening, and I can't be held accountable for that. Kizzy will forgive me, I'm sure she will."

"If I wasn't one-hundred percent sure you weren't in the house, I'd say you had a pretty good motive to get rid of Charmaine."

"Of course it wasn't me. But Charmaine ground everyone down. We all had reasons, motives. Excuses, even."

At this I raised a disapproving eyebrow. There were few excuses for murder. "Do you plan on telling Heavenleigh?"

At this, Saffron blew out her cheeks. "I have to at some point. Not today, though. I guess I should be happy. I've never had a real sister before."

"I think you have six close sisters already, even if you aren't related."

Saffron grinned. "You're right. That's a lovely way to look at it."

"Besides, real sisters can be complicated. Trust me."

A door clicked open down the hall behind me and I turned around to see Maya poking her head out. "There you are, Saff. Get in here, we've been waiting for you."

"I'm coming," Saffron replied over my shoulder, then she turned her focus back to me. "Thank you for talking that out with me, Poppy. I'm coming to terms with all of this. Probably not the best day to bring in extra emotions. There's been a lot swirling around in my head."

For a moment I stared at her. I couldn't understand what it was that had caught my attention, couldn't understand what had given me a sinking feeling in my gut. *Was it something she'd said?*

"Are you okay?" she asked.

I nodded as the sinking feeling settled. My mind had finally clicked it all into place. I knew who it was. I knew who killed Charmaine. Steeling myself, I followed Saffron into the bridesmaids' chamber and locked the door behind me, prepared to lay it all out on the proverbial table.

Fifteen

THE WOMEN SCURRIED about, adjusting hair, straightening their hemlines, clipping errant threads.

I scanned the room from side to side, taking in the pre-wedding flurry. There was Saffron, the bride, in her airy-fairy dress and head full of crystals. Kismet, the once-scorned bestie and now Maid of Honor. Clover, the entrepreneur, whose kombucha empire teetered on the precipice. Ziggy, splayed in a side chair, eyes bleary from drink. Heavenleigh, the commune princess and kleptomaniac. Jennifer, the college dalliance, somehow still beige even in her seafoam gown. And finally, Maya, the yogi doctor, fit and strong and keeping them all together. They were a motley crew, but as Saffron had said, all sisters in the end.

They hardly noticed my presence and carried on with their activities. After a minute, Heavenleigh must have spotted me because she called me over to help stitch a broken seam in Clover's dress. "Just hold it right there," she said with a needle and thread clenched between her teeth. "I've almost got it."

Clover's dressed saved, I retreated to the door and turned to the women. I cleared my throat to grab their attention. Nobody stopped. I cleared my throat again, this time with a much louder "Ahem!"

At this, they stopped and turned toward me. I stood before them like a teacher, and they were placed side-by-side like a police lineup. *How fitting.*

"I want to congratulate Saffron and Chad. I hope you have a joyous marriage full of love and laughter."

"Thank you, Poppy. That's so sweet of you."

"And for the rest of you, I have some bad news."

Their faces went from smiling and friendly to wary. They looked from one another to me, trying to puzzle out what I meant.

"Charmaine's killer remains on the loose," I said. "Walking among us. Laughing among us. I'm sure each of you have wondered who it could be. Or perhaps you chose not to care. After all, Charmaine was a bad apple." I met Saffron's gaze. "Maybe she deserved to die."

Saffron's eyes dropped.

I continued, "But others needed her. She was their lifeline." Eyes shifted to Clover. "A necessary evil."

Clover moved her weight to her other foot, also avoiding my gaze.

"For some, it was personal."

Kismet raised her chin defiantly.

"For some, she was the root of all their vices."

Ziggy dabbed at a bit of drool at the side of her mouth.

"And for the others," I said, "she coveted your most intimate secrets."

Jennifer gulped.

"She collected them like small treasures."

Heavenleigh clasped her hands together tightly in front of her.

"Charmaine knew a secret about nearly everyone. I suspect she knew one about you, too." I shifted to stare directly at the woman at the end of the lineup. "Isn't that true, Maya?"

Maya inched back a step. The others stared dumbfounded, but I matched her, moving closer. "What secret did Charmaine have over you, I wonder?"

Maya shook her head, but said nothing.

"Charmaine was a strong woman. It would take someone just as fit to take her on. An athletic yogi, perhaps?"

"You can't be serious?" Kismet said. "Maya was the one who tried to save Charmaine, remember?"

My eyes narrowed. "Are you sure about that? Did anyone check? Does anyone else know CPR?"

Mouths worked, but no one came up with any dissent.

"But she was in my room," Heavenleigh said.

"And how do you know she stayed there? You admitted yourself that you left and were downstairs, busying yourself with *things*."

"Well, she was there when I got back."

"Again, that doesn't mean she didn't leave after you and return before you."

Maya's eyes shifted to the door, but I stepped between it and her.

"Maya," Saffron said, "tell Poppy this is all nonsense."

"There's one last thing." I stepped forward and gently lifted the necklace from Maya's neck. "This is quite lovely, but I'm sure I've seen it before. On Charmaine, in fact."

Maya pulled away and grasped the necklace with both hands. She looked around at the others, worry in her eyes.

"She wore it that first day," I said. "Along with a pair of earrings. Yet, when we found her on the floor, the jewelry was gone. I found it hidden in your room, but assumed it had been taken by…someone else." I was about to say Heavenleigh's name, but decided to save her the embarrassment. "There was a look between you two—you and Charmaine. Something about that necklace caused you to react."

A sorrowful glance by Maya at the necklace around her neck told me I was right. "It was my late mother's. It's all I have left of hers." She ran a hand over the delicate gold chain.

Clover asked the question we were all wondering. "Why did Charmaine have your mom's necklace?"

Maya slumped into a nearby chair and shut her eyes. "I do have a secret, and Charmaine found out. I'm sure Poppy's already figured it out so I'll let her tell you."

This could go very sideways. If I was wrong, the moment would be ruined, Maya would call me a charlatan, and the others might decide I've lost it and kick me out of the room. I ventured my guess anyway. "You're not a doctor, are you?"

The others erupted at my accusation, but Maya just sighed her acknowledgement of the truth.

"You refused to prescribe any medication, you spend

all your time doing yoga, and you didn't jump into action when Charmaine was on the floor. I called you 'doctor' but you rarely responded."

"It's hard to say how it happened, really." Maya clutched at her mother's necklace. "Charmaine found out I'd dropped out the first semester of medical school. She threatened to tell the others if I didn't give her the necklace. She's always wanted it." Maya scowled. "Just another jewel in her crown."

The others shared uneasy glances. I'm sure they must have understood what Maya meant by that. They'd all been mistreated by Charmaine—used, blackmailed, lorded over.

Maya continued, "She wore it that first night just to rub it in. To remind me that she'd won. Charmaine always wins. I'd regretted it immediately, giving her the necklace. In a moment of weakness—or fear or shame, I suppose—I'd let her intimidate me. I didn't want all of you to find out I'd failed. It was humiliating."

Saffron walked over and gave Maya a hug, careful not to scrunch her dress. "You'd never be a failure to us, Maya."

Agreement followed from all the women, even Jennifer, who'd barely known the woman.

"Motive aside," I said, "you've now admitted it was you. I suspect you snuck into Charmaine's room once Heavenleigh was no longer a factor."

Maya nodded. "I'd also overheard Saffron telling Kismet she'd be sneaking out, so I knew she'd be alone. I wanted to ask Charmaine to return my necklace."

"I'm guessing she said no."

"She said more than that. Not only did she refuse, but

she threatened to tell everyone anyway as punishment for trying to go back on our arrangement."

"Sounds like Charmaine," Kismet said disdainfully.

"I guess something came over me," Maya said. "Maybe it was fear or shame again, but the thought of losing my mother's necklace and being humiliated was too much. I didn't mean for it to happen. I was so enraged. She was...infuriating."

The others nodded, and I spared them a frown. *Were they going to let Maya off the hook for murder?*

"It was almost too good a chance to pass up. I could get the necklace back and eliminate Charmaine's looming threats once and for all."

A knock sounded at the door, then the handle jiggled. "Is anybody in there?" Harper's voice was a welcome relief.

When I unlocked the door, she poked her head in and seemed to notice the awkward silence in the room. She whispered to me, "Is everything okay? Everyone's waiting."

I leaned close so only she could hear. "Would you fetch Deputy Todd and tell him I've got the killer in here with me?"

"He's not going to like that *at all*." Harper grinned like mad. "I'll be right back."

I turned back to the women only to find they'd crowded around Maya and were consoling her in soft whispers and gentle pats on the shoulder. Instead of interrupting, I let them continue. It wouldn't serve me to be on the long end of the moral stick, but the short end of their ire.

The door burst open and nearly knocked me aside.

"What the heck is going on in here?" Deputy Todd shouted. Then he spotted me. "You!"

"Calm down," I said. "I can explain. It was an accident."

He let out a raspy hoot. "The murder or your ceaseless interference?"

I knew this dressing down was coming, but it seemed more important to unmask the killer. "My interference." I pointed to the dark-haired woman in the chair. "She's the one."

He didn't move. "I don't take orders from you, Miss Lewis." Instead, he approached the gaggle of bridesmaids and they stepped back, leaving Maya alone in the chair, eyes downcast. "Now, this insufferable girl"—he indicated me with a jab of his thumb—"seems to think you're guilty of murder. What say you?"

Maya simply nodded.

His eyebrows shot up. "What? Are you sure?"

She nodded again.

"All right, then," he said, tossing a glare my way. "That's good enough for me." He pulled out his handcuffs and fastened them to Maya's wrists.

Ziggy began to sob, then the others followed suit, tears dribbling down their faces.

"We love you, Maya," Clover said.

Heavenleigh nodded. "We'll always be by your side. Sisters forever."

Deputy Todd rolled his eyes as he led Maya away. He stopped just before me. "I've got my hands full now, Miss Lewis, but you're to stay put until I return. Do you hear me? I don't want you leaving this church."

I stammered, "But I've got to help with the reception

across the street. Angie needs me."

"Tough luck, buckaroo. That's what you get for messing with my business. Now I get to mess with yours." His eyes darted up to my head, and a smarmy grin spread across his face. "Nice hat," he said before he disappeared through the door.

I groaned. Angie was going to be devastated, and I was stuck in this church with a group of ladies who'd just lost one of their sisters, thanks to me. They hadn't seemed to notice I was still there. *Must be the shock*.

"What are we going to do now?" Jennifer finally asked. "There's a church full of guests waiting for us."

Saffron swooned and plopped into the chair vacated by Maya. "This is all too much to take."

Kismet rushed to her side and fanned her with a scrap of paper off the desk. "We carry on, that's what."

"Carry on?" Clover repeated in a wavering voice. "How?"

Heavenleigh was the first to speak. "We do what Maya would have done." She took in a deep breath. "Meditative breathing exercises."

Nods all around. They quickly gathered into a circle in the center of the room, a bride and her five bridesmaids, and inhaled and exhaled in perfect rhythm.

With the women distracted, it was the right time for me to escape. I slipped out the door unnoticed and relieved that justice had prevailed. Deputy Todd could take it from here, for better or for worse. I could sit back, relax, and enjoy the wedding with nothing sinister hanging over my head.

***

I returned to the nave where I found my friends seated together with Ryan. As promised, he wore his kilt. After the encounter with the bridal party, I needed that kilt more than ever.

As I took my seat next to Ryan, Harper leaned over. "How'd it go?"

"Harper told me you called for Deputy Todd," Angie said. "What happened?"

"Deputy Todd?" Ryan asked. "You aren't getting in the middle of his investigation are you?"

"The middle?" Harper laughed. "She's the whole of it."

I gave Ryan an apologetic smile and looped my arm in his.

"Well?" Harper urged.

"It was Maya, the yoga instructor."

Angie gaped. "Not the yogi? Her class was so gentle and relaxing. How could she be a killer?"

"Years of pent-up resentment and bullying can drive a person to do unthinkable things, no matter who they are. Oh, and she's not a doctor."

Angie's mouth gaped wider.

Ryan joined her. "She was pretending to be a doctor and she murdered someone?"

I patted his arm. "I know. Shocking. But it's all over now."

"Yeah, Ryan," Harper said. "You're a bit late to the party on this one. You know this is like, the billionth, murder Poppy's solved, right? And you're only surprised because she claimed to be a doctor?"

"Aye." He nodded mindlessly, eyes drifting off. "I guess it caught me off guard."

Angie cleared her throat. "Like Poppy said, it's all over now, so we can sit tight and be thankful that no more murder is in our future."

Harper nodded toward me. "And you're sitting here with us, so I assume the wedding is still a go?"

Angie gasped and clutched my arm. "It's still on, right? All that work on the food…"

"Yes, yes. Saffron still wants to go through with it." I gestured to the full church. "We're all here anyway, there's no point in calling it off."

Angie settled into the pew. "Phew. I was worried there for a second."

I gulped. "There is one thing."

Angie's eye twitched.

"Deputy Todd asked me to stay behind because he has questions for me, so I won't be able to make the reception."

"Not make the reception?" Angie repeated the words like bricks.

"Don't worry. You'll still have Harper, Lily, and Greta." I motioned toward my sister and housekeeper who sat further down the pew. Greta twiddled her fingers at Angie.

Angie's face fell even further. "I guess we'll have to make do. It's not like you could let a murderer get away with it."

"I'll try to be as quick as I can."

The bride was overdue, but we sat patiently. My small crew knew the reason, at least, which made the delay less annoying. I couldn't say the same for the faces near the front of the church. Beige heads would turn occasionally and strain to check the hallway leading to the preparation rooms, as though that would speed things up.

I squeezed Ryan's arm. "I'm glad you and your kilt were able to make it."

He raised an eyebrow and side-eyed me. "I hope it's a better gift than a musty old book about houses."

"You aren't still upset about that, are you?"

He pushed his glasses further up the bridge of his nose. "I couldn't let that upstart bookstore fellow overshadow me, could I?"

I grinned and lay my head on his shoulder. "Your kilt is a lovely gift."

"Just for you," he whispered.

Angie leaned in. "Benjamin Locke came into the bakery earlier today. I asked him about all that noise and he chalked it up to construction, but I don't know why he insists on working late at night. And Lovie said she's seen trucks there really late. Shelby and I saw one there last night, too."

"How long does it take to open a bookstore, anyhow?" Harper asked. "Do you think he's cooking drugs or something?"

I frowned, disappointed in both of them. "I'm sure he just wants to get it right, especially since this town can be so *judgy*." My emphasis on that last word clammed them up. I inched closer to Angie and Harper so no one else could hear. "Are we still on for after the reception? If I'm clear of Deputy Todd, that is?"

Angie groaned and sank lower into the pew. "I don't know, Poppy. I'm going to be running on fumes by then."

Harper shrugged. "I was hoping to meet up with Charlie at some point."

I couldn't believe what I was hearing. "Don't you

want to find out what secret Claude's been hiding in this church?"

"I mean, yeah," Harper said, "but I also want to meet up with Charlie."

"This is the perfect opportunity," I said. "We'll have free reign of the place."

Neither spoke up.

"What happened to our sense of adventure?"

"For the record," Angie said, "I have never had a sense of adventure."

"I *am* on an adventure," Harper said. "It's just with Charlie this time."

"I can't believe you two would leave me high and dry." I gave them my best disappointed glare.

Angie shriveled, but Harper rolled her eyes and crossed her arms tightly across her chest. "Fine," she said, "bully me into it."

"I don't think that's fair," Angie said. "We agreed to help Poppy. Besides, if I remember correctly, it was you who pushed us to snoop around here. You're always bullying me into these adventures, except when it gets in the way of your own plans."

Harper's lip stiffened.

Angie lowered her voice even further. "Remember when you urged us to go to Prosperity so you could find some gold doubloons? Remember how that turned out? The Gold Hand goons almost caught you both down a well, and I had to save your sticky buns. It could have been a disaster. Cho and her crony came within ten feet of discovering you, and then who knows what would have happened?"

I shivered at the memory. Harper and I had both been

perched precariously down a dry, crumbling well in the middle of an abandoned forest town, fearfully straining to hear the voices of the dangerous Cho, one of Everett Goodwin's right hands, and a man, both unseen, inching toward our hiding space. Only Angie's quick thinking had saved us from discovery.

The first light note of music played and Angie, Harper, and I sat up from our whispered discussion.

"Finally," Lily said loud enough from the end of the pew for those around us to hear.

One by one, the bridesmaids entered and made their way along the aisle toward the front and took their places opposite the groomsmen.

My stomach turned. Once again, something had given me a terrible sinking feeling. I scanned the bridal party. Bridesmaids and groomsmen. Women and men. Angie's previous words struck me. Cho and her crony. Cho and a man.

My eyes widened just as the first chord of the bridal music played. I nearly choked at the revelation. Wedding forgotten, I grabbed the attention of Harper, Angie, and Greta.

"What's wrong?" Angie whispered, eyes flicking to the bride as she glided down the aisle.

"Angie just mentioned that time in the forest where we were trapped by Cho and someone else—a man."

"Don't remind me," Harper said. "I still have nightmares."

"That man," I said. "We never saw him, did we?"

"I wasn't there," Greta said. "The three of you went alone."

"You know I didn't see him," Harper said. "I was

trapped down that well with you."

"I didn't see him, either," Angie said. "I was hiding behind a redwood."

"We heard both their voices. We knew Cho's, but the man's voice was new."

"Yeah," Harper said, "so what?"

"We *have* heard it."

Angie blinked. "We have?"

"Yes," I said. "It's Benjamin Locke."

Harper slapped a palm to her forehead. "Of course! That's why he seemed so familiar."

"Oh my gosh." Angie fluttered and fell deeper into her seat. "I thought he was someone I'd run into in Vista and that's why I couldn't place him."

"I couldn't place him either," I said. "But when I think back, the voices match. Benjamin Locke was hunting us down in that forest alongside Cho."

"You know what that means," Greta said. "The Gold Hand is already here in town."

Angie stared up at me, still dazed. "But why would the Gold Hand want to open a bookstore?"

Greta grunted. "If that's a bookstore, then my grandmother was a flying circus monkey."

"Angie," I said, "you said you saw a truck out front and that Lovie mentioned seeing it before?"

She nodded. "And lots of noise."

Ryan tapped gently on my shoulder. "Is everything okay? The wedding…"

"Sorry," I whispered in response. I sat back and tried to catch my breath. Benjamin Locke was part of the Gold Hand. I couldn't believe it. I'd flirted with him! The memory of my fluttering eyelashes and saccharine voice turned my stomach. When I remembered he'd gifted me a book about Claude Goodwin's house, my face reddened from how blind I had been, and I squirmed in my seat. I'd fallen for his ruse hook, line, and sinker. I looked at Ryan, who stared forward toward the ceremony at the front of the church. I'd acted a fool all while I had a perfectly wonderful man by my side already.

Greta caught my eye from down the row. She mouthed the words "Let's go" and bobbed her head toward the exit.

The timing wasn't great, to say the least. Saffron and Chad stood together at the front of the church, and Pastor Basil's hippy-dippy voice wafted over us like a haze of second-hand smoke. Then there was Ryan. He held his hand in mine, but with the other I was itching to go. Benjamin Locke could be up to anything, and the bookstore was right across the street. He was yards away at this moment and my anger seethed, urging me toward action.

I gauged the pros and cons of the situation, then I remembered Deputy Todd was on my back. If he knew I'd left, I'd be in hot water up to my eyeballs. But my frown turned into a sly grin. I'd learned something else earlier. Sisters look a lot alike, and I had one conveniently seated just a few spaces down the pew. How many times had Lily been mistaken for me and vice versa? A plan formed in my mind. *It might actually work.*

Decision made, I dipped my head toward Ryan and whispered, "I need to leave for a few minutes."

"Is everything all right? How long?"

I patted his hand. "Don't worry about it. I'll be back." Scooting along the pew, I gathered Harper, Angie, and Greta. "Follow me," I said when Angie looked at me questioningly. I slid in next to Lily on the pew.

She eyed me sideways from beneath the brim of her designer hat. "What?"

"I need you to do something for me. Wear my hat."

"Don't be absurd."

"I really need this favor, Lily."

Her arms crossed languidly across her chest.

"You owe me this much," I said. "All I need you to do is wear this hat and don't let the deputy get too close to you."

She pulled the hat off my head and rubbed the thick fabric between two fingers. "Is this synthetic?"

"I have no idea. Will you wear it? Just for a little while. It would mean the world to me. And this is only something *you* can do." It took every ounce of power to beat down my ego for the next three words. "I need you."

Lily shifted in her seat. "I suppose it couldn't hurt. It's not like these wedding photos will be in any glamour magazines." She undid the pins that held her own delicate hat on and set it aside. Then she placed my synthetic hat atop her head, slightly askew, placed just right and secured it with the pins. "Not for long," she said. "Don't forget."

I breathed a sigh of relief. "I won't."

Harper, Angie, Greta and I scurried down the end of the pew and disappeared out the door.

Once outside, Angie screeched to a halt. "What are we doing? What about the reception?"

"You're the one who insisted now was the time to help Poppy," Harper said. "You don't get to skip out now."

"We don't know how long this will take," I said. "We

may be back in time. But first, we need to find out what the Gold Hand's been up to in that musty, boarded-up bookstore."

Sixteen

WE RACED ACROSS the street, Greta lumbering behind in her oversized pants. The bookstore was quiet at this time of day, but the windows remained covered. I peeked through the tiny corner of upturned paper, but no light came from within, leaving the entire shop shrouded in darkness.

"Do we just break in?" Harper asked.

Angie leaned over and started inspecting the area around the doorway. "Maybe there's a key hidden somewhere in these—"

The sharp crash of breaking glass cut her off.

We looked to the bookstore's door. Greta, extra-long caterer sleeves bunched around her fist for protection, reached through the now-broken pane and unlocked the door.

"Add that to the list of misdemeanors," Harper said.

"Let's go and hope no one heard us." I gave Greta a disapproving glare, but time was short, and her methods were effective.

The door swung open. Shards of glass tinkled as the door pushed them aside. I stepped through into the first large room. The paper that had blocked the door's light now hang limply to the side, casting a line of sunlight into the bookstore. My shadow loomed long, and I urged everyone inside and to clear away from the door so as not to block the light.

It was evident that the bookstore was nowhere near ready to open. In fact, it looked like nothing had been touched since the old owner sold the business. The mismatched wooden bookshelves still lined the walls. The same genre titles were taped to the top of each shelf. History. Art. Architecture. The memory of Benjamin gifting me the book ran through my mind again, but I shook it away.

"What's all this?" Harper's voice was incredulous. "It looks exactly the same, only with worse lighting."

"Is there more to this store?" Greta asked. "Somewhere hidden?"

Angie pointed toward a side room, off from the main room and behind a closed door. "Office," she whispered.

I waved for them to stay back and stepped forward. I pressed an ear to the door and listened for any hint of a sound. Nothing. Nodding, I waved them forward and opened the office door.

It was the smell that hit me first, like wet dirt. The light from the storefront didn't reach this far, so the office remained dark.

"Musty," Harper said.

"What is it?" Angie perched on her tip toes trying to see over Harper's shoulder.

"I can't see, it's too dark. Something is definitely off

here."

Suddenly, a bright overhead light flickered on. I turned on instinct, ready to face a foe.

Greta's finger still lay on the light switch. "Use your noggins, would you?"

Harper, Angie, and I let out a collective sigh of relief. The tension was running high.

Harper pointed into the office. "Look at that!"

With the room now fully lit, the source of the smell became clear. Floorboards had been ripped off and cast aside, and in the middle of the room, a large hole had been dug into the earth.

"Who would dig a hole in a bookstore?" Angie asked. "That's so strange."

I stepped close and leaned over the hole. "Not a hole. A tunnel."

Harper groaned. "Not another one."

"Where does it go?" Angie asked.

My eyes followed the line of the tunnel from the entrance of the hole. Sure of what I would find, I rushed to the office window and ripped down the stifling paper. There, across the street was exactly what I suspected—the Fellowship of the Faith church and Claude Goodwin's final resting place. "They're after the treasure," I said. "Benjamin Locke has been digging a tunnel straight underneath the church."

"Right under our noses," Angie said with a wail. "How sneaky!"

"What do we do now?" Harper asked.

"You don't mean to go down there, do you?" Angie looked from Harper to me. "Remember what happened last time you two went down a dark tunnel?"

"Yes," Harper said, "I remember since you reminded me of it just a few minutes ago."

Angie grabbed a hold of my sleeve. "You can't be serious? I'm beginning to suspect Benjamin Locke's interest in you wasn't quite honorable, Poppy. What if he's down there waiting for you with a gun? Or worse, Cho? She's shot at us before. I had to hide in the backseat of your car and I was scared out of my wits. We can't go through that again. We don't know what's down there. I've got a wedding to cater!"

I bit my lip, weighing our options.

"Where's Greta?" Suspicion formed Harper's words.

I looked to the tunnel. "Oh no."

From the depths, Greta shouted back, "No lollygagging. We've only got one chance, and I don't intend to be left behind again."

***

I lowered myself into the musty dirt tunnel and stared down the length before me. A string of tiny lightbulbs had been run from an outlet in the office and strung along shoddy wooden struts erected along the length of the tunnel. They made it just bright enough to follow the way.

Harper followed after me, then assisted Angie down the hole. She let out a low whistle once she got a look at the tunnel. "What an operation."

"Benjamin must have been working hard," I said. I ran my hand along the first wooden strut. "There's a lot of effort behind this. He must have been hauling the dirt away with those trucks."

"There's no chance he did this alone," Greta said. "There aren't enough hours in the day."

The implication was clear. "That means there could be more Gold Hand operatives at the end of this tunnel."

"I don't like the sound of that," Angie said. "Why are we down here again? Is this a good time? Maybe we should come back later."

But Greta had already started down the tunnel, forcing me to follow her. While she maneuvered with purpose, Harper, Angie, and I took our steps more tentatively, sure that at any moment Dr. Everett Goodwin or Cho or some boogeyman would jump from the darkness at overtake us.

"Where do you think we are right now?" Harper whispered, looking upward at the rough tunnel ceiling.

I looked back at the fading light from the office hole. "I'd gauge somewhere under Main Street. Does anyone have a light?"

Harper patted her hands on her hips. "No pockets on these stupid catering uniforms, remember?"

Angie clung to Harper's arm. "Where do you think this will come out?"

"Directly underneath the church," I said. "Look, the tunnel gets smaller up ahead." The walls of the tunnel closed in, forcing us to hunch over. The gouges in the dirt were rougher as well, as though the burrowing became more frantic.

Greta called back to us, "They must have realized we were getting close, and it lit a fire under their butts."

At about the point I guessed we'd crossed onto church land, the space had narrowed so much we moved in single-file. Something caught my ear and I stopped. "Can you guys hear that?"

"What?" Harper asked. "All I hear is Angie's heavy

breathing."

"I hear it too," Greta said. "Music?"

"It must be from the wedding. We're probably directly under the church right now."

"Oh no," Angie said. "Shelby will wonder where we are."

"She's still got Mason and Lily to help her out. Don't you want to find out what's at the end of this tunnel?"

Angie shook her head emphatically.

"Well," I said, "you can't turn back now."

"Yeah," Harper said, "and you wouldn't be able to climb out by yourself, anyway."

"Shh!" Greta hissed. "I hear something else."

I held my breath, and I was sure my friends were doing the same. Then I heard it too, faint at first, but then the rhythmic sound became clearer. "It's the ocean."

"How can we hear the ocean underground?" Harper asked.

"Waves crashing can be pretty loud," I said, "but I'd expect it to be muffled. This sounds too clear. And do you smell that?" I sniffed the air, once musty from the dirt now held a hint of salty sea air.

Greta wiggled her nose. "This tunnel must open up to the ocean or to caves along the cliff face."

Harper scoffed. "There's no way Benjamin Locke—or whatever his real name is—dug an entire cave to the open ocean."

"He didn't," Greta said. "Water crashing against the rocky cliff for millennia has probably carved out a huge cave system underneath the town."

"Keep your eyes open," I said. "If this singular tunnel is going to open to a maze of caves, I want us to be on our toes."

The sound of crashing waves grew louder and the scent of the sea grew stronger. The crude walls of the cave appeared wet from the misty spray of the ocean.

We progressed slowly and silently. With no sign of the Gold Hand yet, we knew they could be just a few steps away. Soon, the dirt walls of the tunnel transitioned to crushed rock and widened, opening into a space the size of a small room. Unlike the rough tunnel, the walls were smooth rock, weathered through the years from a gush of water that sprayed through a number of eroded holes in the floor.

"Is the ocean under us?" Angie whispered.

I nodded. "Wave erosion. We must be in a cave on the cliff's overhang. There're more openings over there." I pointed toward the uneven side of the room where slick fissures led to additional eroded spaces.

I took one step toward one of the fissures, intending to slip through, but stopped when I heard a man's voice from within. I held a hand out to stop the others from following me and they halted.

"We should use the axe," a familiar man's voice said.

A messy clank of metal followed.

I turned to my three friends and mouthed "Benjamin."

"And who?" Harper mimed.

The next voice answered her question. "I know what I'm doing," Cho said. "This saw will make quick work of it. Why don't you go shovel some dirt or something?"

I crept to the wall of the room and peeked through a small fissure into the adjacent cave. A sturdy wall of aged brick was embedded into the dirt wall, half exposed from recent excavation. Benjamin stood nearby, arms folded, looking irritated. He watched Cho, who knelt with the saw tool in hand and protective mask down, working intently on her target. Debris from the saw shot out and a grinding squeal pierced through the cave as it cut through the bricks.

I had no doubt what was behind that thick wall—Claude Goodwin's tomb and treasure. I scurried back to my friends and mimed what I had seen.

"What do we do?" Angie whispered in the faintest voice.

I glanced at Greta, who looked ready to spit nails.

"There are only two of them and four of us," I said. "If we take them by surprise, we might be able to overtake them."

Harper held out her hands, palms forward. "Hold on. Four of *us* is about half a person each. Two of *them* are like double. That makes it four against two, but the opposite way, and I don't like those odds."

From seemingly nowhere, a knife appeared in Greta's hand.

"How did... Where did that come from?" I asked, bewildered.

"Always come prepared." Greta gave the blade a long, appreciative look. "Thought it might be handy during the reception, so I stowed it away in the folds of this prison uniform."

"Handy?" Harper repeated. "For what? Holding up the guests at knife point?"

"I don't suppose anyone else brought a weapon?" I asked.

Harper and Angie shook their heads.

"At least we have the element of surprise. They're not expecting us, and they're not looking in our direction, so we can sneak up from behind if we're quiet."

Harper gave Greta's knife a wary glance. "Maybe someone else should take that."

As quickly as it had appeared, the knife disappeared into the generous folds of Greta's catering uniform, putting an end to that conversation.

I motioned for us to move, and as a group we approached the fissure and I checked on Benjamin and Cho once more. Cho continued cutting, engrossed in her task, but Benjamin must have grown bored. He paced the cavern aimlessly, dodging the numerous drips from the ceiling that spattered onto the slick floor. We'd have to watch our step. This place was dangerous.

I scanned the rest of the cavern. Another opening on the far side must lead to yet another water-carved cave. Without direction, someone could get really lost down here.

Benjamin finally turned around, pacing back toward Cho with his back turned to us. The sound of the saw filled the cavern. Now was our chance. I waved a hand for the others to follow and slipped through the fissure into the adjoining cave. Careful to keep my steps light, I scurried closer to the two Gold Hand operatives. I spared a glance back toward Greta, who held her knife at the ready. For some reason, it looked much smaller now that our ambush was underway.

Benjamin stood watching Cho, hands in his pockets. For all I knew, he also had a knife. Or a gun.

I didn't wait until he turned around. "Stop what you're doing," I shouted. The unexpected echo within the cavern startled me.

Benjamin turned, but Cho, mask on and saw sparking, appeared not to hear.

Greta jabbed the knife toward Benjamin, swishing and darting it back and forth.

Still a few feet away, he gave it little heed. Instead, a smug grin appeared on his face. "You finally made it. Took you long enough."

"I should have known you were up to something." My face grew red hot as shame boiled to the surface.

He shrugged.

By now, Cho had noticed us and tipped up her mask. The noise from the saw ceased. Her face was as disinterested as Benjamin's, as though they'd expected us all along. The only twinge of emotion on her face was a quick glance at Harper. I was sure Harper remembered her fleeting crush on Cho and now felt the same shame and anger I felt.

"How nice of you to join us, Poppy Lewis."

As a group, my friends and I turned. Dr. Everett Goodwin stood at the fissure, blocking our way back. He held a gun steady in his hand and stared directly at me. Angie began to snivel and pressed up against my side. Greta had backed away from Benjamin and closed ranks with Harper, Angie, and me.

Dr. Goodwin waved the gun at our party. "And to bring your friends for the occasion. How considerate."

Harper leaned in to whisper, "Poppy, I don't like this math at all. It's six against two now, even with Greta's paring knife."

I agreed. The math just got a lot worse and our exit had been cut off.

Everett Goodwin used the gun to wave Benjamin toward us and the taller man stepped forward.

I grabbed my friends and pulled them toward the gap I'd spotted earlier. We rushed for the opening. My first step slipped, but I quickly regained my footing. Greta scurried through first, followed by Harper. I pushed Angie into the gap but she got stuck. A hard tug by Harper popped her through, and I followed, just as Benjamin got a hand on my wrist. I wriggled under his firm grip, but couldn't free myself. From beside me, a glint flashed off Greta's knife as she swept it across Benjamin's forearm. With a howl, he finally let go and we rushed down a slick corridor, anywhere away from our pursuers, but I knew Benjamin and the others wouldn't be far behind.

The roar of crashing waves grew louder as we followed the tunnel. A faint hint of daylight was enough to make our way. *Where was the daylight coming from?*

The answer soon became clear as the tunnel opened to a huge cavernous space. An opening of crumbled rock and dirt to the right let in the light. But what drew my focus was an oblong hole in the center of the cave floor, carved from centuries of ocean waves and opened to the sea below. In the tightened quarters, I spied a pile of sharp, fallen rocks piled far below. Spray from the waves misted up into the cavern with each wave crash, making the cave damp and slick. The sound was deafening.

I ran to the far side, searching for another corridor, but there were no other openings. We were trapped. I pushed the others behind me and we crowded away from the giant hole bursting with seawater.

From the other tunnel, three figures emerged. Benjamin first, followed by Cho, then Everett Goodwin sauntered into the open space, gun still in hand.

"No where to go," he said with a sneer. "I think it's time you finally got what a thief deserves."

"Thief?" I repeated. "What are you talking about?"

He laughed. "You don't even know, do you? Pathetic little innkeeper living your pathetic life. Small, insignificant. I thought I'd spelled it out for you, but I guess you're too thick to see it."

"See what?" I asked. My eyes darted around the cavern, looking for anything that may serve as an advantage.

"You think you're entitled to Atticus Goodwin's gold."

"You mean Claude Goodwin's gold. And everything points to me." The message scrawled in Atticus Goodwin's tomb came back to me. *'Only those born of golden blood may possess the riches borne from blood.'*

Everett spat. "Claude Goodwin stole that treasure. My line is the true heir to Atticus Goodwin's fortune."

"Who cares?" Harper shouted from behind me. "He was a pirate. It was *all* stolen to begin with."

"Your ancestors were sullied," Everett said. "That house, the gold, the fortune, it all belongs to me. I'm here to take it back and you're in my way." He gave one nod to Benjamin and Cho, and both made their way around the vent in the center of the circular cave, careful to keep to the edges.

"What do we do?" Angie wailed. She tugged at the back of my black catering shirt. "I'm never going to see Roy again!"

I held my hands out, protecting my friends as Benjamin and Cho moved closer. Greta wiggled her knife in preparation, and Benjamin scowled. He held one hand to the cut on his forearm, eyes burning fire at Greta.

Our options were limited. We could stand and fight. According to Harper's math, we were down six against two. I'd wager Everett Goodwin's gun counted for about twenty more on their side. The other options were even less inviting. Throw ourselves into the sea via the geyser within the cavern, or out the opening of the cliff side, where nothing but ocean and rock and certain death would greet us. I steeled myself for a fight.

Harper hopped from foot to foot, readying herself for action. She could probably hold her own, but the thought of my friends fighting for their lives cut into my heart.

"I don't know what you're doing, Benjamin, but you don't have to do anything rash. We're no threat to you."

"Tell that to the cut on his arm," Cho said with a sneer. "We should have taken care of you a long time ago, but Dr. Goodwin wanted to play games."

We were backed against the wall now with nowhere to go. Benjamin and Cho had corralled us into a slippery alcove and inched closer.

My arms were outstretched to the sides, keeping my friends back, but from beneath one arm, Greta lunged, knife waving frenetically. Benjamin dodged the first swipe but slipped and took a knee. Cho grabbed for the knife. Greta moved like lightning, twisting away from Cho before jabbing her once in the shoulder. The woman let out a vicious wail and grabbed at the wound. Regaining his footing, Benjamin kicked at Greta's hand and the knife went spinning across the wet and uneven floor, coming to rest well out of reach while Greta fell to the floor from the force of the attack.

Dr. Goodwin laughed from across the cavern. His

maniacal smile made more sinister through the spray jetting from the eroded opening in the center.

I reached for Benjamin and grabbed him by the shoulders trying desperately to pin his arms down. But the man was too strong. He quickly overpowered me and spun me around, then pushed me into the cavern wall and reached for Greta on the floor nearby.

A long spindly leg flung out and smacked him clean across the face. Harper bandied on the balls of her feet, ready for the next kick.

Nose bleeding, arm bleeding, Benjamin had taken a few decent licks, but Cho was back by his side, now equipped with Greta's discarded blade.

"Enough of this." Cho spat on the nearby ground.

Benjamin grunted an affirmative response.

I knew we couldn't keep up our fight much longer. We'd lost our only real weapon, and I couldn't expect Harper to kick us out of this predicament.

Benjamin lunged for me. I pushed against him, but his arms wrapped around mine, pinning me as I'd tried to pin him. I struggled against his grip.

"You let her go, you nasty beast!" Angie beat her fists against his arm. "I can't believe I gave you a complimentary bear claw!"

Harper swung her long leg out behind his knee and he buckled. Cho sprung at us, but Greta had regained her footing and barreled into the woman.

Benjamin let go, and I scrambled to the safety of the cavern wall. He toppled from the force of Harper's kick and latched onto Cho to stabilize himself. But Cho was also unsteady. She'd been pushed sideways from Greta's tackle and spun her arms, desperately trying to find balance.

Then she slipped.

The slickness of the cavern floor seemed like oil underneath her feet. They gave out from under her and she fell back. In that frantic moment, she'd reached for Benjamin, who had reached for her, and together they tumbled backward. As if in slow motion, the two fell as one through the center hole just as a massive wave crashed against the rocks below, spraying a plume of seawater through the gap.

Cho's scream faded behind the roar of the waves then suddenly went silent.

We stood stunned for a moment. Greta heaved from her effort and Harper had stopped bobbing from foot to foot. Angie held her hands over her mouth, her big blue eyes shone in horror.

I stared at the hole, equally horrified at what had just happened, then I turned my gaze to Dr. Goodwin, who remained safely on the other side of the cavern, gun still casually aimed in our direction. "This didn't have to happen," I shouted through the spray. I held up my arms in defeat. "What now? Are you just going to shoot us?"

A glimmer of irritation crossed his face. "Not yet. You can still prove useful and open my vault."

Harper stepped forward. "Do it yourself, you slimy git."

He held up the gun. "I could do without this one."

I quickly placed myself in front of Harper and held out my hands. "Wait. We'll do it."

"But I don't know how to open a vault." Angie's tiny voice was barely a whisper behind me.

"It's okay," I told her. "We'll think of something."

"Yeah, something," Greta growled.

We inched our way around the circular cavern, keeping to the walls. As we approached Dr. Goodwin, he stepped aside, careful to keep plenty of space between himself and our party of four. He motioned for us to take the long tunnel back to the cave with Claude Goodwin's bricked-up tomb and treasure.

We passed him single-file. Angie first, then Harper, me, and finally Greta, whose intense scowl made even Dr. Goodwin flinch.

Just as we'd entered the tunnel, a gigantic roar sounded behind me. I turned in time to see Greta lunge at Dr. Goodwin. The tiny woman must have taken him by surprise. He raised his gun, but it was too late. She was upon him, scratching at his face like a rabid old hag.

"Greta!" I shouted.

Harper and I rushed toward them, but Greta's attack had pushed Dr. Goodwin to the edge of the chasm. They fell and grappled on the slick ground, Greta fighting like a bulldog and Dr. Goodwin fending her off but unable to maneuver the gun into place. They were right on the edge. Too close. Harper tried to kick the gun from Dr. Goodwin's hand but missed as he flailed his arm in defense.

Then it happened, in one move, Dr. Goodwin rolled off the edge of the hole. In the melee, Greta slipped after him. I watched helplessly as she disappeared over the edge. My heart stopped.

Seventeen

HARPER LUNGED, SLIDING to the edge of the hole and grabbed ahold of the small woman's bony hand. The old woman dangled precariously. I watched in horror as Harper, flat on her stomach and straining to hold on to Greta, began to slide toward the edge herself. Without thinking, I leapt forward and grabbed onto Harper's ankles. She was heavier than I expected, but then again, she was holding onto Greta over the edge. I braced myself as best I could against the jutting rocks, but with the slickness of it all, I wasn't sure how long I could hold her.

"Pull me up!" Harper shouted. "I've got her."

"He's got my legs," Greta's gruff voice shouted from below. "He's pulling me down."

I realized Dr. Goodwin must still have ahold of Greta, dangling below her, all of us connected like a chain. I struggled to maintain my grip on Harper's legs. Every second felt like an eternity and every moment felt like she'd slip through with the slightest movement.

"Pull me up," Harper shouted again.

"I can't!" I grunted as I chanced to adjust my grip. "Too heavy."

"We need to lose this dead weight." The sarcasm in Greta's voice came through the bursting sea spray clearly, without a hint of distress.

My face, straining with the effort, dripped with salty water, but I held fast. Laying headfirst toward the chasm, my foot had caught against a jut in the floor, and I braced myself as best I could. I knew I couldn't hold them for long. Already, the muscles in my legs fought against me.

Hands clasped around my ankles. Angie! But it wouldn't be enough. Together, we began to slide toward the blowhole.

"I can't do it," Angie cried. She hugged my ankles tighter, but we continued to slide, inch-by-inch.

My hands ached from the effort of holding onto the cascade of bodies. I cursed myself for forcing my friends into this trap. And for what? A bit of gold. Some excitement? In that moment of holding my friends' lives in my hands, I'd had enough excitement to last me a lifetime.

"Hold on, Poppy!" Angie pressed all her weight against me, trying anything to stop our slow progression towards doom.

"Get off me, you lummox," Greta shouted.

The pull on my arms increased, and I slid another foot toward the gap. *Was Greta swinging down there?* My face was inches from the edge. If I went over, surely Angie wouldn't be able to stop us all tumbling to our deaths.

Another jolt pulled me close enough to the edge that I could see below me. Harper's thin body extended below. My fingers were like a vise around her rainbow-socked ankles. She held Greta's wrists with her long, spindly fingers, and below her, Everett Goodwin clung to Greta's ankle with a single hand. His face was no longer smug. Instead, he grimaced at the effort of holding on. Greta's oversized pant leg must have made it even more difficult.

"He's got me by the cuff!" Greta shouted.

I readied myself for one more tug, but I was quickly losing steam. Suddenly, just as the sea spray died down between waves, a loud snap echoed throughout the chamber. Even at my awkward angle, I watched as Everett Goodwin broke from Greta's ankle and fell toward the sea far below, the broken remnants of an ankle monitor following his path. His scream rose, then was lost as the next wave crashed up through the hole.

Then the clear cackle of Greta's laughter flowed up to me as she swung precariously below us. "Hallelujah! He stole my tracking device."

The relief of Everett Goodwin's fall was short-lived. The tug on my arms, although lessened, still felt too heavy to bear, and I knew my fingers would slip. They were numb from the cold and from my desperate grip on Harper. Frustrated, tears welled in my eyes. *I can't lose them!*

Angie yelped as her hand slipped from my ankle.

I began to slide. Fast. In that moment, with the sight of the ocean roiling and writhing below, and my best friends facing a gruesome end, time seemed to stop. Images of their smiles flashed before me. The first time I met Harper while sitting on the porch stairs at the Pearl. Angie's kindness and hospitality that first night when I had no heat or electricity and no place to stay. Greta, knobby and uncouth, but a treasured member of my found family, nonetheless. And Ryan. Sweet, wonderful Ryan, whose unwavering love and loyalty had been my rock in the toughest of times. It was Ryan whose visage stabbed hardest at my heart. *Would he find my body? Would we ever be found?* I imagined the grief, the loss, and felt it in my heart in that brief second before I would surely tumble over the edge.

In that darkest moment, a strong arm grabbed me at the shoulders. Confusion overtook me as I slid backward, away from the gap. Then a soothing Scottish brogue, like sunlight through rain clouds, told me everything would be all right. "I've got you," Ryan said. "I won't let you go."

Ryan! My Ryan!

Still face-down, he dragged me farther away from the craggy hole and soon Harper emerged, still clinging to Greta for dear life. Finally, my tiny old housekeeper scrabbled back from the edge to safety.

Tears of joy and exhaustion streamed down my face. Ryan wrapped me in his arms and I cried deeply into his shoulder. Harper lay flat on the ground, arms and legs splayed out, breath heaving. A relieved smile spread across her face. Angie rushed to her side, fidgeting and checking that she was still in one piece.

Greta stared at the gaping hole grinning like a cat. She let the water crash over her as the waves broke. "What a rush."

I couldn't help but to laugh through my tears. We'd made it. We were okay. I glanced up at Ryan and a rich sense of love overtook me. I didn't care about my tears or that I was smeared with the muck of the cavern. I pressed my lips against his and knew I'd never let him go.

Eighteen

OUR RELIEVED SILENCE was broken by Harper's boisterous cackle. "I can't believe I almost jumped to my death to save Greta. It was like a reflex."

Angie wrapped her arms around Harper. "Well, I'm glad you did. And I'm glad Poppy saved you, too."

"And I would like to thank the late Dr. Goodwin for freeing me from my tracking device." Greta wound her ankle in a broad circle, taking in her newfound liberty.

I squeezed Ryan tighter. "What happened? Why are you down here?"

"You left so suddenly, I had to see where you were going. I watched you enter the bookstore and debated following."

I stared up at him, confused.

"But then a man entered the bookstore a few minutes later. It wasn't Benjamin, but I didn't like the look of him, so I had no choice except to follow. It took me a while to find the tunnel." He stared around at the cavern in wonder. "What's been going on down here? Where is

Benjamin Locke?"

I held out a shaky arm. "Can you help me up?"

Ryan lifted me from the ground and I stretched out my arms and legs. They continued to ache from the effort of holding onto my friends. I let out a great sigh.

"Who was that man I followed?" Ryan asked. "And where is he now?"

Harper and Angie averted their eyes and said nothing. Greta suddenly showed great interest in a loose thread on the cuff of her sleeve.

"It's a very long story," I said. "Can I fill you in later?"

"No more secrets," he said. "You'll tell me everything?"

"Everything," I said. "And right now, I can at least show you something."

As a group, we hobbled down the long tunnel back to the cavern that held the exposed brick wall. The equipment remained on the floor where Cho had discarded it.

Harper rushed to the wall of the tomb and felt around with her hands. "It's as solid as the rocks of this cave. No wonder they were having to use this stuff to get in."

"What is that?" Ryan asked. "And who was breaking in?"

"That," I said, pointing at the brick wall with a broad smile, "is my inheritance."

"Your inheritance?" He seemed even more confused. "And someone was trying to break into it?"

"You're soft, Dr. MacKenzie." Greta strode to the tomb with intent in each step. "You have no idea what lurks in the shadowy underbelly of this quiet seaside town."

Angie looked at me, perplexed. "Starry Cove has a shadowy underbelly?"

"She means there are—were—bad people trying to steal something from me."

"And they were down here?" Ryan asked. "That was the man that followed you?"

"Yeah," Harper said, "except there were two more jerks trying to take us out, too."

"Take you out?" Ryan shook his head, disbelief on his face.

"Like I said, I'll fill you in later. Right now, I want to try to find a way to break into this encasement."

"How do you suppose we do that?" Harper asked.

"We may need to go fetch a—" I stopped as Greta knelt down and fit Cho's helmet to her head. She picked up the masonry saw and hefted it in her hands.

"Let's see what this puppy can do." She popped down the face shield and flicked the trigger, then held the tool to the jagged scar left behind by Cho. Greta picked up where she'd left off. It was slow going, and we had to avert our eyes from the flying debris as Greta work diligently cutting out an entry point.

"What is that wall?" Ryan asked.

"I'm fairly certain that is the tomb of my great-great-great-grandfather."

"His *tomb*?"

"That's right. He built the Pearl, and we think he's hoarding his fortune within that box."

"Wait," Ryan said. "Isn't this graverobbing?"

"No, it's—" I frowned. *Was it?*

"Of course not," Harper said with confidence. "He practically invited us to break in, right Poppy?"

"Yes," I said slowly. "Something like that. He set us on a mission, and that mission led us here." I gestured toward the encasement emerging from the dirt walls.

"Why do you want to break into a tomb?" he asked. "What's inside that thing?"

"We have no idea," Harper said. "But if it's not heaps of gold, I swear I will throw myself through that hole back there."

Angie plopped onto the ground, exhausted. "I'm just thankful that Dr. Goodwin won't be bothering us anymore."

Ryan looked at me as if he were going to ask who Dr. Goodwin was, but I held up a hand. "Later."

The whirring of the saw died down, bringing our attention back to Greta. The first cut had been made, and she was already on the tips of her toes, reaching to make the next long horizontal incision.

I turned away as the saw fired up again and let my thoughts wander to what could be on the other side of that door. It could be a lot of nothing, like Atticus Goodwin's tomb was when Harper and I descended into his underground lair. *But what if it isn't?* All signs pointed to this being the end goal, the final resting place, no more riddles and side quests. *This has to be it.*

We waited patiently, which must have been torture for Harper, who I was sure tingled in her boots at the prospect of finally reaching Claude Goodwin's supposed treasure vault.

At last, the final cut was made. We rushed to Greta's side as she tore off the helmet.

Harper placed her fingers against the edge of the cut-out section of brick and pushed, but it didn't budge. She kicked it and pushed again.

"It must be thicker than we thought," I said to her "We'll find a way."

Greta paid no attention to Harper's tantrum. Instead, she stepped into a darkened corner and emerged with a long axe. "Looks like our friends were kind enough to leave all their tools."

Harper perked up. "I can help with that."

She heaved the axe against the sturdy brick cutout. Once, twice, she struck the bricks, breaking off chunks with each swing. On the third swing, the axe broke through.

A stale, musty air whooshed out from within and was quickly dissipated by the cool ocean air. My heart raced.

Harper quickly finished breaking through the remaining bricks.

"Who goes in first?" Angie asked.

"Poppy should go," Greta said. "It's her ancestor after all."

They all nodded and I couldn't help but grin with excitement. I rubbed my hands together. "Okay, this is it."

The opening was slim, and I had to shimmy to get through the crumbled bricks into the darkness beyond.

The light from the Gold Hand's artificial lights cast only a faint sliver into the chamber. "I can't see anything," I called back to the others. "Pass me one of those lights."

A moment later, Greta slid in after me, holding one of the lanterns aloft. The unnatural light illuminated a small chamber, perhaps ten feet long and wide, casting odd shadows off the opposite brick walls. My eyes adjusted to the flickering light and a moment later, my jaw nearly hit the floor. Filling the room, in some places floor to ceiling, were toppling stacks of shiny gold and silver coins, smelted gold bars of varying sizes, piles of glittering multi-colored jewels and gems—a ruby as big as my thumbnail—and luminescent rounds of lustrous pearls. It was more than I could have ever expected. I could have swum through the rivers of riches filling the space.

Harper let out a low whistle behind me. She was stuck half in and half outside the crypt, and stopped short once she caught sight of the gold. "Holy cow." She slapped a palm to her forehead and let out a gigantic peal of laughter. "Finally!"

"What is it?" Angie pushed and pulled and tugged herself through the tiny opening. Her eyes went wide at the sight of the abundant riches lining the walls and strewn across the floor. "Oh my gosh. Is this real?"

I bent down at picked up one of the gold coins. Turning it over in my hands, I couldn't believe it myself. They were real Spanish doubloons, heavy and imperfect. Even after how long they'd been hidden in this lightless crypt, they gleamed like the day they were cast.

"There's gotta be, like, a million dollars in here."

"More," Greta said, almost breathless. "Much more." She bent down to her knees and ran her gnarled hands over the treasure. "We did it, Arthur," she whispered. "We did it."

"Poppy?" Ryan eased through the opening. His kilt caught on the remnants of the ragged cut edge of brick, and he tugged to free himself before turning to the group. Then he saw the contents of the room. "What the... *This* is your inheritance?"

"Uh-huh." I nodded at him with a grin. "It's real."

He fumbled for his phone in the leather pouch hanging atop the front of his kilt and turned on the flashlight feature. The room instantly grew ten times brighter.

With the space fully illuminated, I spotted something else in the room. Propped upon a stone plinth in the far corner lay the distinct shape of a marble coffin. It appeared plain and dull against the shimmering gold and silver and jewels filling the vault.

I stepped forward and lay a hand on my ancestor's marble sarcophagus. "You didn't make it easy," I whispered.

"Look there," Harper said, pointing toward the side of the coffin where a delicate script had been carved. "*Only those born of golden blood may possess the riches borne from blood.*"

"That's you, Poppy," Angie said. "The heir who figured it all out."

I scanned the room one more time, ready to pinch myself at the absurdity of it all. Then I looked to my friends in turn. Harper, Angie, Greta. "Only with the help of my dearest friends." I spread my arms wide, and they met me in the center of the room for a hard-fought embrace.

As we separated, Harper asked, "What do we do with all this stuff now?"

"Hey," Ryan said, calling us over to one of the walls. "Does this look like an opening to you?" He pointed toward a distinct line that broke the plane of the wall.

I ran a finger down a long crack that ran from ceiling to floor. "Yes, I think there's…" I pushed against the wall and it gave way with the grinding of stone on stone. A set of carved steps led upward. Another false wall greeted us, and I pushed against it as well, expecting the same give as the last one, but it stuck firmly despite my efforts.

"Let me try," Ryan said. He stepped up the wall and pushed his shoulder against it. Nothing.

"Let's all try," I said, motioning for the others to crowd in.

"Can't we stay and play in the gold?" Harper stared longingly at the piles of coins.

"There'll be plenty of time for that," I said. "Besides, what if this leads to more treasure?"

Harper leapt forward, and we all stepped to the wall and pushed our combined might against it. Reluctantly, it inched open with the rough groan of stone grinding on stone. Suddenly, bright, fluorescent light streamed into the small stairwell. A swath of colorful fabric brushed against the false wall and blocked our view of what was beyond.

Angie gasped and pushed forward to the front of the group. "I know that fabric. It's the tie-dyed tapestry hung in Pastor Basil's office."

"We're back in the church?" Harper asked.

"I suppose so." I dipped under the flouncy fabric and into the office space. It was Pastor Basil's office, all right. I turned back to the opening. The enormous tie-dyed tapestry covered almost the entire wall.

"Let's close the wall behind us," Greta said. "We don't want to give away our trail."

Once pushed back into place, it was obvious why this false door hadn't been found before. While the crypt side was stone, the office side matched the wood paneling perfectly. The seams along the walls were invisible, and there were no handholds to pull the door open. Pushing would do no good—it was a one-way hinge.

Harper rounded a desk in the office and surveyed the wall. "I bet that old hippy never knew he was sitting on a mountain of pirate gold."

I checked the wall one more time, running my finger along the invisible seam to ensure it would remain undiscovered. "C'mon," I said to the others. "Let's get out of here before we're found out."

Angie was the first to the office door. "We need to get to the reception. Shelby will be in fits, I'm sure of it."

We exited the office into an empty hall and through to the nave. The hordes of guests were gone from the church, but a few guests still milled about catching up or gossiping, whichever was their penchant, but it meant that the ceremony must have finished recently.

"I hope we're not too late." Angie rushed through the pews and out the front door of the church. We followed close behind, and even Harper with her long legs could barely keep up with our scurrying friend.

"How'd she get so fast?" Harper asked.

Greta huffed in the back, the cuffs of her oversized pants hiked up and bunched in her hands so she wouldn't trip. "Never underestimate a woman's defense of her culinary reputation."

I spared a glance at the bookstore as we ran across the street. With the paper in the windows, it was difficult to spot that the glass in the door had been broken out.

As we expected, Shelby's shriek when we arrived nearly brought the place down. "Heavens dearies, where have you *been*? Mason fell asleep and Daisy snuck in and tried to eat the wedding cake! It's absolute bedlam in here. Your sister's been a lifesaver, Poppy."

I gaped, truly shocked. "Really?"

"I'm so sorry we're late, Shelby." Angie bent over, trying to catch her breath. "Ran into an unexpected delay."

Shelby waved her arms at the five of us. "But where have you *been*, dearies? You're covered in mud head-to-toe. You can't serve canapés looking like that!"

Angie ran a palm down her cheek, then looked at it. She was filthy. She ran the palm on her dark caterer pants, but that made it worse. "Oh dear."

Shelby waved us toward the back of the community center with a flick of a small towel. "Go wash up before anyone sees you."

But before we made it too far, a familiar twang rang through the hall. "I've been looking for you, Miss Lewis."

I spun to face Deputy Todd.

He eyed me up and down with a sneer. "Care to tell me where you've been? You're a mess, and I told you not to leave."

I kept my face calm, even though I knew I looked like I'd crawled through a mud pit before being run over by a truck. "I'm sure I don't know what you mean."

"I'd been following that sister of yours around thinking it was you."

"Oh? That sounds like your problem."

"I know you've been up to something." He waved his hands at the dirt and mud caking my uniform. "Just look at you."

"I fell down." *Technically true.*

"Fell?" He leaned to the side to look at my companions. "All of you?"

"Look here, Mister Deputy," Harper started with her

signature sass, "if you want to—"

"Excuse us, Deputy Todd." Angie pushed forward to stand next to me. She batted her big eyes and clasped both hands in front of her as if pleading. "We desperately need to help with the catering. Could we please be excused to clean up so we can help Shelby?"

"I've got questions for Miss Lewis here," he spat. "Lots of questions."

"And what questions are those?" I asked.

Deputy Todd blustered, blowing out his cheeks. He must have expected me to fight his demands. "You..." He shook his head as if clearing a muddle. "How..."

I raised an eyebrow, waiting for him to continue.

"What... How did... Oh, confound it!" He stamped a boot, and it echoed through the hallway. Then he wagged a stern finger my way. "I'll interrogate you later, Miss Lewis. And don't you sneak away this time."

Nineteen

I SIPPED MY coffee at the small kitchen table, bobbing my crossed leg and smiling at the man seated across from me. "You look cute in the morning."

"Stop, milady," Ryan said. "You're making me blush." He didn't try to hide the smile that spread across his face.

"You're making me blush, too." Greta stirred a pot of oatmeal from atop her stool at the stove. "In fact, you were making me blush all night, and you know I need my beauty sleep."

I caught Ryan's eye, and we both laughed.

"It's a good thing Lily moved into one of the empty suites," Greta said, still stirring with her back to us, "otherwise you'd have heard an earful. That lady doesn't hold back. It's admirable."

"What's admirable?" Lily asked as she swung through the door into the kitchen. "That Poppy finally realized those stupid smart devices were an absolute debacle and got rid of them?"

I glanced at my delicious hot mug of coffee. "I have to admit, I like having my old coffee back. The unburnt toast is nice, too."

Lily let out a brief sigh. "And I was just starting to like this place." She poured herself a steaming mug from the carafe then disappeared back through the kitchen door.

"What did that mean?" Ryan asked, nodding toward the swiveling door.

"It's more than the coffee that's got her in a good mood. Her collection is due out and the early reviews have been pretty good. And she told me she's moving out."

Greta spun on her stool. "Out?"

I nodded, knowing this news would catch Greta by surprise. "Uh-huh."

"Great golly magoo. I'll be nice not to face the chic police every morning."

"You're probably glad to get her out of your hair," Ryan said.

I mused on that for a moment. "Maybe. I think she may come and visit. Once or twice a year sounds like plenty."

Ryan glasses steamed up as he smirked behind the rim of his mug.

Heavy footsteps pounded on the porch outside before the kitchen door swung open.

Harper nodded toward us as she entered, two white pastry boxes held in her arms. "Morning. We brought more cinnamon rolls." She held the door open with her hip while Angie strode in, also laden with boxes from her bakery. Mayor Dewey slid in behind them and jumped onto the table, taking up his favorite spot at the corner where he could observe everything.

Ryan stared at the boxes. "That's a lot of cinnamon rolls."

"Yeah," Harper said, "but these are *special* cinnamon rolls." She popped open one of the lids. Instead of gooey hot pastries, the unmistakable shimmer of gold and jewels filled the box. Once Ryan had a good peek and Dewey had given it a sniff, she closed the lid and dropped it on the table with a thud. The coins and gems inside tinkled. "Oof. This stuff is heavy."

"So that's how you've been getting it all over here," Ryan said. "Very clever."

"Just your friendly neighborhood bakery delivery," Harper said. "Nothing to see here. We've been going down every day and bringing up what we could carry. It's slow going."

Angie stood next to Harper, still holding her own bakery boxes. "Do you want to put those down, Angie? They must be so heavy."

"What?" Angie blinked at me. "Oh, the box." She shook her head and giggled. "It's not treasure. I brought actual cinnamon rolls."

"Sounds like treasure to me," I said. "Your cinnamon rolls are always welcome. Coffee anyone?"

"Yes, please," Harper said. "You don't even have to ask. Er, wait. Is it that smart coffee thing?"

Greta made a chuffing sound from her stool.

"No," I said. "I got rid of all that. Too much trouble."

"How is this treasure transfer going?" Ryan asked. "Looks like you have a system down, but where are you putting it all? I don't think the banks in Vista will accept gold doubloons or raw, uncut jewels."

"It's going in the basement," I said. "There's a little alcove hidden behind a false wall my late uncle built." I thought back to the moment when Harper, Angie, and I had discovered Arthur's secret room. It had held nothing but a journal then, but that journal had started this entire adventure. "It's almost like he knew I'd need it. I'm just sorry he couldn't be here to enjoy it."

Greta sucked in a heavy breath. "He'd be real proud of you, Poppy. Real proud."

"Are you crying?" Harper asked her. "Are those actual tears?"

"No," Greta snapped, turning back to the stove. "Stupid onions."

"Have you thought about what you're going to do with it?" Angie asked. "It's a lot of gold, but like Ryan said, difficult to deposit at the bank."

I shrugged. "No idea. I don't want to horde it like Atticus did. I want to do some good with it. Maybe I can sell a few of the jewels." I slipped a hand in my pocket and pulled out the thumbnail-sized ruby I'd taken from Claude's tomb. I held it up to catch the sunlight streaming in through the window. The shimmer of reflected red light flickered off the floor and bounced to the ceiling, catching Dewey's attention.

"That will get you a pretty penny," Harper said. "Enough to live off."

"And you can sit back," Greta said. "Enjoy your hard-earned rest."

I took a bite of gooey cinnamon roll then sipped my coffee, savoring its richness and warmth on my lips. Mayor Dewey nudged his head against my hand and I gave him a scratch behind the ears. "You're right. I think I'm due for some peace and quiet for once."

The End of Book 6

Lucinda Harrison is a writer and crafter who lives in northern California with her two mischievous cats. She is the author of the Poppy Lewis Mystery series.

Connect online at lucindaharrisonauthor.com

BOOKS BY LUCINDA HARRISON
Poppy Lewis Mystery Series
Murder in Starry Cove
Best Slayed Plans
A Foul Play
Dead Relatives
Shock & Roll
Bridesmaid Blues

Made in the USA
Monee, IL
28 March 2025